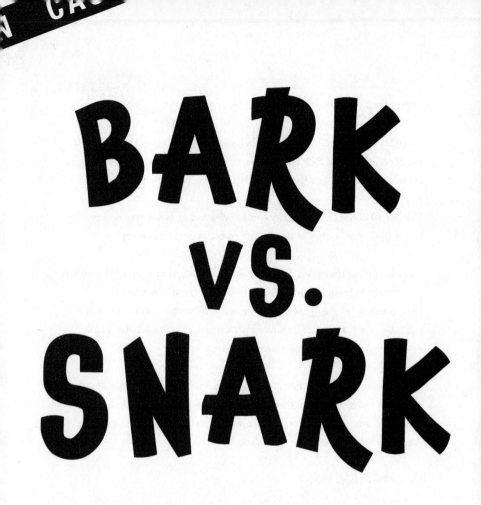

BARK vs. SNARK

A QUEENIE AND ARTHUR NOVEL

SPENCER QUINN

SCHOLASTIC PRESS • NEW YORK

ISBN 978-1-338-24583-7

1 2020

Printed in the U.S.A.   23
First edition, October 2020

Book design by Maeve Norton

FOR GEORGE

ONE

ARTHUR

A H, SUMMER. MY FAVORITE SEASON of the year by far, way better than . . . those other ones, the names not coming right off the bat. And here's something you should know about me: Whatever doesn't come right off the bat, doesn't come, period. So I don't even bother trying to remember! Who needs bother? A life free from bother is the life for me! You should try it! But don't try too hard. Trying too hard turns out to be bothersome all by itself. Nothing's simple, as humans like to say, although it's not the kind of remark I like to hear. I prefer "Who's a good boy?" And "Anyone want a treat?"

On a nice warm summer day like this one, I love to lie under the big shady tree out front, meaning out front of the Blackberry Hill Inn. That's our B and B up in the Green Mountains, very green at the moment, as I'm sure I could have seen for myself had my eyes been open, which they were not. How peaceful to simply lie in the shade, eyes getting a nice rest, but at the same time nose and ears taking in all sorts of things, like the smell of the flowers in the

1

garden, especially the purple ones, which reminded me of Mom's perfume. Mom is not my actual mom, if I'm understanding things right, but I call her *Mom* in my mind. She's the actual mom of the twins, Harmony and Bro. That's our core group here at the inn—me, Mom, Harmony, Bro. Perhaps I should include one other party, but do I have to? The truth is I don't want to include Queenie, so I won't include her or even mention her name.

But what was I thinking about? Quee—that is, the party I'm not mentioning—has a way of knocking me off track. Ah! Summer, that was it! Summer, with the aroma of the apples on the apple tree getting stronger every day, and the cool water smell from Blackberry Creek on every breeze, even though the creek was a bit distant—no way I was going for a walk down there in this heat, although a swim would have been nice, and just floating around even nicer. And what about all the lovely summery sounds—for example, the beating of butterfly wings over my head, and the approaching flip-flop of someone in flip-flops coming from the road? Who? Not just anyone but Bro. I know the sound of Bro walking, no matter what he's wearing. There's also such a thing as the smell of Bro walking, only in the air when he's wearing his old sneakers. When that happens I can smell him from a long long distance, possibly all the way across town.

Flippety flop, flippety flop. Bro came closer.

"Hey, Arthur," he said. "Back in dreamland?"

Dreamland? Certainly not. I opened my eyes, couldn't have looked more wide awake and rarin' to go, although going anywhere was not in my immediate plans. And there was Bro! What a nice sight! Flip-flops, shorts, T-shirt, his face all ruddy from the sun, his teeth and the whites of his eyes so white, his toes dusty. If I had even a bit more energy I'd have licked off that dust. As it was, I just wagged my tail. Actually not, since I seemed to be lying on it.

"Look what I've got!" Bro said, and from behind his back he produced a Frisbee. A Frisbee? Was there something exciting about a Frisbee? Not that I could think of.

He held it closer, maybe giving me a better view. A small-ish Frisbee, bright green, like a traffic light. Green, as I knew from riding in the car, means go. Was there some . . . what would you call it? Connection, maybe? Some connection between the color of this Frisbee and . . . and . . . I got a little lost. But one thing was for sure: I was starting not to like this Frisbee. On a cooler day, I might have considered burying it in the tomato patch.

"Are we gonna have fun with this or what?" Bro said.

Meaning *what* was a choice? If it was, then—

Bro spun the Frisbee into the sky. "Arthur! Go!"

Go? *Go* coming up again, and so soon? Did this have anything to do with me? Where, exactly, was I supposed to go? So many questions! I watched the flight of the

Frisbee—a rather pleasant sight—and told my mind to take it easy. Which was just what it wanted to hear! How did I know? Because right away my eyelids started getting heavy, a sure sign of a mind growing nice and relaxed.

"Arthur?"

What was this? Bro was still around? I love Bro, of course, and was happy to be near him. But did we need a whole lot of back-and-forth right now?

"Come on, Arthur," he said. "We haven't got much time to learn this."

Uh-oh. We were learning something? Not another trick? I already knew one excellent trick called playing dead. A real crowd-pleaser, but Bro hadn't been satisfied so we'd moved on to shake-a-paw, which I never got the hang or the point of. There's only so much learning you can take in this life.

Meanwhile Bro had trotted over to the Frisbee—flippety flippety flop, flippety flippety flop—and was now trotting back. Always a pleasure to watch Bro or Harmony when they're on the move. They're good at sports, especially hockey and baseball. Baseball had just finished, with their team, named the Bobcats, for some reason, winning something or other, possibly the championship. Mr. Salming, the coach, gave Harmony the game ball, which is now in my possession. I keep what's left of it under the padded chaise on the patio.

But back to Bro, now trotting my way, Frisbee in hand.

"Arthur! On your feet!"

Was that a nice way to ask?

He crouched down, scratched between my ears, did a fine job, although too brief. "Come on, Arthur. It'll be fun."

That was much nicer. What a great kid! So great that I came pretty close to getting up. In my mind I sort of did, although my body remained stretched out on the lawn, the short grass soft and comfy, almost like the putting green at the golf course, where it's possible I was no longer welcome. How had that happened? Before I could remember, Mom appeared from around the side of the inn, over by the shuffleboard court, carrying hedge clippers and wearing a kerchief on her head.

"Hey, Mom," Bro said. "How long do you think it'll take Arthur to learn Frisbee?"

Mom came over. Hey! What was this? Bro was somehow now as tall as Mom, or even a bit taller? When had that happened?

She gazed down at me. "Until the twelfth of never," she said. "What are we going to do with you, Arthur?"

Why, same as always—love me to death! No need for any changes. Just keep doing what you're doing.

"The twelfth of never means it's hopeless?" Bro said.

Mom gave him a smile. She's a beautiful woman with real sharp eyes that warm way up whenever she smiles. I could watch her all day and sometimes I do, except for the napping parts, of course.

"Nothing's hopeless," she said.

"Oh, good," said Bro. He took a crumpled sheet of paper from his pocket and handed it to Mom.

She smoothed it out and read it aloud. "'Something new at the county fair—a Frisbee-catching contest for dogs! Show the folks what your pooch can do. No entry fee and lots of prizes, including a year's supply of ChewyChewChews, the best chewy around, and a brand-new mountain bike for the winner's human.'" She glanced at Bro. "The fair starts on Tuesday."

"So we have three whole days," said Bro.

"That's the spirit," Mom said. "Come on, Arthur. Dig deep." And she headed off toward the hedge that borders the road, the clippers over her shoulder.

"Mom?" said Bro. "The mountain bike sure would be nice."

"I hear you," Mom said, not looking back.

Bro turned to me. "Arthur? What are you doing?"

Interesting question. I seemed to be up and on my feet, and not only that, but digging what looked like the beginning of a quite deep hole in the lawn. There's a kind of digging where you use just the front paws, but for big jobs you want to get the back ones involved, too. And I was getting the back ones involved, oh, yeah, baby, involved and good, clumps of earth flying this way and that, blades of grass scattering away on the breeze, and even a wobbly earthworm or two, probably with surprised looks on their faces, if they had faces, which I really wasn't sure about. But who cared? What fun this was, digging, digging, digging. Thanks to Mom, for giving me the go-ahead. Dig, Arthur, dig! Dig all the way to—

"ARTHUR!"

TWO
QUEENIE

A RTHUR!"

What now? Do I ask for much? No, not me. Who could be more undemanding or easier to live with? All I want from life is a little peace and quiet. But now, somewhere outside but not nearly far enough away, we had Bro shouting a name that gets shouted fairly often in these parts.

By these parts, I mean the Blackberry Hill Inn and surrounding property. It's a beautiful inn—which you probably guessed, since it's mine, and I'm all about beauty. The inn is not mine alone, of course—I'm happy to share it with the rest of the family, meaning Mom, Bro, and Harmony. Bertha the cook is also on board—she's in charge of pouring my fresh cream into my special china saucer, known as Queenie's saucer, after which she whips up breakfast for the guests. It's possible we haven't had enough guests recently—I've caught a worried look on Mom's face a few times—but what would be the point of me worrying about it? My job is to concentrate on, well, me. Me and me alone, and only me. But it can be hard to concentrate when—

"ARTHUR! STOP! WHAT GETS INTO YOU?"

What gets into Arthur? An interesting question. Bro was not alone in bringing it up. I'd asked myself the same thing, and was now asking it again, as I glided down from the top of my grandfather clock across from the front desk, where I could keep an eye on all the comings and goings at the inn, and moved in my lovely silent way across the hall, past Mom's desk, and onto a filing cabinet next to a window with a good view of the front yard.

And there, in the shade of our giant tree—an oak, if I'd heard right, and I always do—we had a Frisbee lying on the ground; Bro gazing down at Arthur; and Arthur, standing in a deepish hole, his face dirty, one of his misshapen ears drooping down, the other sticking out weirdly to the side, gazing back up at Bro and panting a bit, like he'd just run a race. Not that Arthur had any racing experience. He's not built for running. He's built more for . . . well, what, exactly? I was trying to come up with something when I heard Harmony approaching behind me. No need to look. I could tell by the soft pat-pat of her bare feet on the wooden floor, her smell, like our meadow after the rain, and from just how the feel of the whole room changed.

"There you are." Harmony came up beside me. "What's so interesting?" She looked out the window. "Ah," she said. I watched her watching. Is there a more beautiful human than Harmony? The way she stands so straight, and her glowing skin, and her big brown eyes, full of golden glints and every bit as sharp as Mom's. Yes, a thing of beauty in her own right. Although not quite in my class. I hate to say it, but I don't want any misunderstandings between us, you and I.

We watched the scene under the big tree, me and Harmony. Bro went to the toolshed, returned with a shovel. By that time, Arthur had climbed out of the hole and was lying on his side, eyes blank. Bro filled in the hole, picked up the Frisbee, held it for Arthur to see, if in fact Arthur could see anything at that moment.

"It's simple," he said. "I throw the Frisbee. You catch it and bring it back. Are we good?"

"I wonder what he's saying," said Harmony.

I glanced at her, just shifting my eyes, head staying still. I have graceful ways of moving and graceful ways of not moving. But that's not the point, which was all about being reminded once again of the weakness of human ears. The thin sheet of window glass was all it took to keep Harmony from hearing the goings-on outside. You had to feel bad for humans sometimes, although I never actually did. Are they my responsibility? Not in the least. My responsibility, as you must know by now, is me.

Meanwhile Bro spun the Frisbee in the air. "Go, Arthur, go!"

Arthur remained absolutely still. The Frisbee glided in a long curve and landed softly on the lawn. Bro picked it up, showed it to Arthur again, and said, "Try just watching. I'll show you how."

Arthur, eyes still blank, thumped his tail on the ground. Bro flicked the Frisbee again, an easy motion that sent it gliding on another long, smooth curve. But this time, Bro took off after it, legs churning, flip-flops flying off. What a nice runner he was! For a human, of course. It's something of a miracle they can even stand up in the first place.

The Frisbee sailed toward the toolshed and began dipping down to earth. Bro sped up, his hair—uncut so far this summer and on the longish side—streaming behind him. Then, just as the Frisbee was about to touch down, he dove, fully stretched out, and snatched the spinning thing out of the air with one hand.

"Wow," said Harmony.

Bro landed, somersaulted, and trotted back to Arthur, a big smile on his face. "There. See how it's done?"

The answer was almost certainly not, what with Arthur now curled in a comfy ball, eyes shut tight.

Harmony backed away from the window. "You and I are going to have an easier time, Queenie."

Oh? For a strange moment I thought—but how ridiculous—that Harmony was about to propose something having to do with me, her, and Frisbees. Instead she took a neatly folded sheet of paper from her pocket, straightened it out, and read, "'Calling all cats! Come to the county fair for our first annual cat beauty contest! The winner gets a year's supply of catnip and a state-of-the-art scratching post! And for your human pal, a brand-new mountain bike! No entry fee! All you have to do is look your best!'"

Harmony gave me a careful once-over, head to tail. "It's in the bag," she said.

Who was I to disagree? There's no hiding from the truth.

THREE

ARTHUR

G O, ARTHUR, GO!"

When Bro says go, I go, you better believe it. The green Frisbee soared into the sky, and I soared after it, my paws hardly touching down. Good luck, Mr. Frisbee, with ol' speedy-legs Arthur on the trail! Mr. Frisbee sailed over a park bench, curved around a tree, dipped down under a bridge, hitched a ride on a freight train, zipped into the open window of an office tower, and zoomed out through a window on the far side, but it was all for nothing, because I, Arthur, did all those things, too. And more! The look on Mr. Frisbee's face when he glanced back and saw me right on his tail? I was still enjoying that sight as I snatched him out of the air, spun on a dime, and charged back to Bro. By that time there was a huge crowd in Yankee Stadium, clapping and cheering. I trotted to the center of the field, letting everyone get a real good look at me. A chant rose up. "AR-THUR! AR-THUR! AR-THUR!" How nice of them! I pranced round and round the stadium, Mr. Frisbee securely between my teeth, my tail raised high.

"AR-THUR! AR-THUR! AR—"

Ding.

What was that?

Ding.

The crowd went silent.

Ding.

Ding? That ding reminded me of the bell on the front desk at the Blackberry Hill Inn. But I was nowhere near the inn. Wasn't I on the mound at Yankee Stadium? I tried to take a good look but saw nothing! Oh, no! What was happening to me? Then my eyes opened all by themselves.

And there I was, not exactly on the mound at Yankee Stadium. Much more like on the floor in the front hall of the Blackberry Hill Inn, curled up as though I'd been napping. Which I would certainly never do! Not in the middle of a busy day. Don't forget I'm in charge of security here at the inn. This was no time for play. I opened my mouth to let Mr. Frisbee drop out, but there was no Mr. Frisbee, although his plasticky taste lingered on my tongue for a moment or two.

Ding.

My gaze went to the desk, where a stranger with a suitcase was dinging the bell with the tip of his finger. Strangers are very much my business. I barked a low bark, not threatening, but just to make my presence known, the presence of someone you don't want to mess with. I could handle Mr. Frisbee and I could handle you, fella. But . . . but had I actually handled Mr. Frisbee? Or . . . or . . .

The stranger slowly turned my way. I've seen lots of humans, but never one who looked quite like this. An older sort of guy most likely, to judge from his shaggy white eyebrows and wild white hair, but his face didn't have much going on in the way of wrinkles, and his teeth were bright white.

He gazed down at me, then spoke in a deep, booming voice. "You won't get far on your looks."

That was baffling. I had no need for going far—or anywhere, for that matter. I was right here, at home. Poor guy, kind of out of it. I decided to put him in the picture. I rose, gave myself a quick head-clearing shake, and made my way over to my white-toothed friend. Hey! He was wearing tassel loafers. I hadn't seen tassel loafers in some time, but I had fond memories of the tassels themselves, especially their nubbly mouthfeel. I lowered my head, got my lips pulled back, and—

And the front door opened and Mom came in, a dirt smear on one cheek and a potted plant in both hands.

"Oh, hello," she said. "Is anyone helping you?"

"Not so you'd notice," said the man. All of a sudden he sounded kind of old, his voice thin and scratchy.

"Well, now I'm here, so—Arthur? What are you doing?"

Me? Why, nothing, nothing at all. I backed away from

those tassel loafers double-quick, my tongue possibly gliding over the toe of the shoe but completely missing out on the tassel itself. Life is full of frustrations. You just have to find a way to deal. I lay down in the nearest corner, and found to my surprise that the tip of my tail was lying quite close by. Almost saying, "Gnaw on me." What a stroke of luck! Lucky strokes are how to deal, in my experience. I got busy on my tail.

"Don't mind Arthur," Mom was saying to the white-toothed guy. "He means well."

Of course I did! Many thanks to Mom for pointing it out, but that didn't stop the man from shooting me a glance that might have been a teensy bit on the unfriendly side. There must have been some mistake. Doesn't everybody like ol' Arthur?

"So what can I—" Mom began.

"I want a room for five nights," the man said. "A quiet room, far from"—he glanced my way again—"any disturbance."

"Do you have a reservation?" said Mom.

He gazed around the front hall and raised one of those shaggy white eyebrows. "Do I need one?"

There was the tiniest pause before Mom spoke. She pauses like that sometimes. I have no idea what it means, but it always gets my attention.

"It's usually better," Mom said, "but in this case we do have the Daffodil Room available."

16

"How much?"

Mom said some number I missed. Numbers are very missable in my experience, and maybe in yours, too. The man handed over his credit card. What is a credit card? I have no idea, but they always get passed back and forth when a guest checks in. I know the routine, better believe it! Could I run the front desk all by myself? Wow, what a thought!

"Welcome, Mr. Ware," Mom said, handing him a key. "I don't know if you have any interest in county fairs, but ours starts tomorrow."

"I have no interest in county fairs." He picked up his suitcase and headed toward the broad staircase that led to the guest rooms on the second floor. The suitcase gave off a very faint smell of cotton candy. I'd only come across cotton candy once before, and that was on my one and only visit to a Halloween party, sometime in the past. A very short visit, possibly because of an incident involving me, my nose, and a big vat of cotton candy. The point is I know the smell of cotton candy. Smells I know can sort of pull me along. For example, the smell of cotton candy was now pulling me to my feet, across the hall, and up the stairs, close behind Mr. Ware. When he came to the door of the Daffodil Room I was right behind him. He unlocked the door, went in, kicked the door closed with his heel, a heel that just missed my head. But who's luckier than me?

There I was in the Daffodil Room, hot on the cotton candy trail.

Meanwhile Mr. Ware didn't seem to be noticing me. He heaved his suitcase onto the bed in one easy motion— pretty good for an old guy—and then opened it and took out a black cloth bag, made, as I knew right away from the smell, of velvet. I forgot all about cotton candy and started concentrating on velvet, which is lovely for both licking and chewing, as you may know already. Also velvet doesn't stick to your nose like cotton candy. I made a big decision, then and there: velvet yes, cotton candy no.

Mr. Ware took the black velvet bag to a small table against the wall, the kind of table with a mirror for putting on makeup. He sat down and gazed at himself in the mirror, actually seemed to be staring into his own eyes. That gave me a bad feeling, so I was glad when he stopped doing it and reached up, maybe to pat his wild white hair into place.

Only that wasn't what happened! Instead he reached his fingers deep into the whole white mess and . . . and pulled it off! Oh, no! He'd pulled off all his hair? That must have hurt so bad! Once I'd had a little incident with my tail and a pot of superglue, so you can trust me on this.

But Mr. Ware did not seem to be in any pain. He sort of folded up his hair, still somehow in one piece, like the whole patch of skin underneath had come off, too—oh, how horrible!—and shoved it into the velvet bag. That was when I saw that Mr. Ware hadn't lost any skin from his head, now covered in dark hair, cut very short, and not bleeding or anything like that.

He went back to gazing at himself in the mirror. How strange he looked! Was he thinking the same thing? Was he about to say, "How strange I look," and put his hair back on?

Mr. Ware did neither of those things. Instead he reached out and pinched the end of one of his shaggy white eyebrows between his finger and his thumb and . . . and ripped it right off his face! Again no cry of pain, no blood. Underneath the shaggy white eyebrow lay another eyebrow, not shaggy, and brown in color. Was Mr. Ware going to rip that one off, too? At that moment I wanted to be out of there. I glanced at the door, but it was shut tight. Once Bro had tried to teach me how to turn a doorknob with my front paws, but that ended up being a little too hard—I had to stand on only my back paws at the same time!—even though he promised me a whole sausage the instant I got the knack. Should I mention that somehow that sausage found its way into my mouth later that same day? Life is good at the Blackberry Hill Inn.

Although maybe not in the Daffodil Room. This new Mr. Ware, again staring at himself in the mirror, was kind of scary. I wanted the old Mr. Ware back. The old Mr. Ware's face wasn't quite so hard. Was this a good time to sidle a little closer, let him know I was on the premises and now wanted out? I was just about to do that when Mr. Ware ripped off his other white eyebrow. He put both eyebrows in the black velvet bag. That was when I was hit by a memory, a sort of tremendous one: I'd see this dude before. I mean the younger one. He'd stayed at the inn some time ago. How long ago? That was a tough one, not the kind I'm good at answering, so I didn't even try. Why make yourself unhappy?

But the point was I'd seen him. I don't forget a face. And even if I do, I hadn't forgotten this one. And here was something amazing: He'd been wearing tassel loafers that time, too! Tassel loafers stick in the mind. Not only that, but a bunch of mountain bikers had been staying with us at the same time. Mr. Ware and Harmony and Bro watched them ride off early one morning, right on the front step, where I'd been at that moment, real close to those tassel loafers. Harmony had said, "Would I love a mountain bike or what?" And Bro had said, "Are they expensive?" "Oh, yeah," Harmony had told him.

Wow! What an interesting day I was having, just staying in my own mind. And then came an interesting question. How come he'd turned himself into the old Mr. Ware? I waited. No answer, meaning it was another tough one, and you already know how I handle tough ones.

Meanwhile he was fishing around in his velvet bag, and soon pulled out a small red squishy sort of ball. Balls are always interesting. You can play fetch with them, of course, which would be so much better if humans did the chasing, but there's also simply chewing on a ball to one's heart's content, always a good way to pass the time. Was there a chance Mr. Ware would now notice me, hand over the ball, and open the door so I could leave, taking the ball with me? Yes, there was every chance! It was about to happen for sure!

Instead something happened I'd never dreamed of. Most of my dreams are about food, although sometimes I dream about napping, but that's not the point. Mr. Ware took that soft squishy ball and stuck it on his nose!

A loud, high-pitched, possibly even frightened bark seemed to shake the walls of the Daffodil Room. Mr. Ware's head whipped around in my direction. He didn't appear to be barking so it had to be me. There you see a little something about how I roll. Even though I was possibly the slightest bit frightened—although fear is something that never ever gets into the heart of ol' Arthur, except if something really scary is going on—I could still keep a cool head and figure out who was doing the barking. Wow! I can be pretty impressive, as maybe you hadn't known. But now you do!

Mr. Ware rose from the stool he'd been sitting on and came toward me. "What are you doing in my room, you dirty dog?"

Whoa! First of all, I lived here! Maybe not in the Daffodil Room, but certainly in the inn, and the room was in the inn, so . . . I lost the trail of where I was heading, but then I remembered the second of all. Dirty dog? He'd called me a dirty dog! No way! We have a little pond in back of the old barn, and Bro and Harmony had shampooed me in it just the other day. I couldn't have been cleaner! Who likes to be called dirty when they're clean? Not me, my friends. I barked right in Mr. Ware's face, really let him have it.

Mr. Ware's eyes narrowed in a mean way. And then he reared back on one foot and . . . and kicked me with the other one! I leaped out of the way, lightning fast. Actually the lightning-fast part—and maybe the whole leap—happened only in my mind. But Mr. Ware's kick missed anyway. Was he expecting me to be lightning fast? Had I outthought him? Ha!

"Go on," he yelled. "Git."

He strode to the door and flung it open. I trotted out, in no particular hurry, the clear winner. But wouldn't you know? Mr. Ware tried to kick me again! This time he got me, although not squarely, more like his foot brushed my side. Which made his tassel loafer fly off! I ran toward it, but Mr. Ware, turning out to be pretty speedy himself, got to the loafer ahead of me and snatched it up. As he did that—a real quick bend and snatch—there was a big and possibly very nice surprise. His red nose ball fell off and bounced down the hall toward the stairs. Do you waste time thinking in a moment like that? You do not! You race after that ball, you grab it, and you take off for parts unknown.

Which was exactly what I did.

"Stop!" hissed Mr. Ware. "Get back here! Heel!"

Heel? Was that one of the commands I was supposed to know? Before I could get a handle on that, I heard Mom calling from downstairs.

"Arthur? What are you doing up there?"

Well, it was kind of complicated. I glanced back. Mr. Ware's face was not a pleasant sight. I had to admit to myself that he might not be a fan. Holding the tassel loafer in one hand, he backed into the Daffodil Room and closed the door. At the very same moment, Mom appeared at the top of the stairs.

"Arthur? What's in your mouth?"

Why, nothing! Nothing was in my mouth. That was my first reaction. And then my mouth sent me a message: It was holding a ball, namely Mr. Ware's red nose ball. What luck! I darted past Mom and down the stairs.

"Arthur!"

Down the stairs I went! From behind I heard Mom's knock. "Mr. Ware? Everything okay?"

"Yes," said Mr. Ware, now speaking in his scratchy old man voice.

"Has Arthur been bothering you? I think he has something in his mouth. I hope it wasn't yours."

"I'm fine. And busy at the moment."

"I won't bother you," Mom said. "Call the desk if you need anything."

No answer from Mr. Ware. By that time I was in the front hall, sprinting toward the door. It happened to be closed, and I was realizing that was going to be a problem, when suddenly it opened and in came Elrod, the handyman, carrying a surprising number of big paint cans in his huge hands. He saw me and I saw him, both of these sightings a little on the late side.

"Arggh!" Crash! Bang! Bangitty bang-bang, that bangitty bang-bang being the paint cans. Were the lids not quite securely fastened? This was no time to hang around. I ran out the door, headed for the backyard, zoomed past the shuffleboard courts, and finally came to a stop in the tomato garden, completely out of breath. But on my in-breaths, I took in the lovely smell from all the fat red tomatoes hanging on the vines. Hmm. Those tomatoes reminded me of something. What was it? I thought and thought, and just when my head was starting to hurt, it came to me: the red nose ball! And would you believe it? There it was, still in my mouth! Wow! Without another thought, I buried it nice and deep in the soft brown earth of the tomato patch.

FOUR

QUEENIE

THE HOUSE WAS QUIET, A SPECIAL sort of quiet that only happens in the middle of midsummer nights. I'm fine with quiet. In fact, the center of the quiet is me, the quietest thing around. Not thing. I shouldn't have said thing. I'm no thing. I'm . . . how to put it more accurately? Accuracy is important. I'd never want to mislead anyone. I know you'd be upset to think of me as a thing. And I care about your feelings! Even if they're rather predictable and boring, if you'll allow me to be honest. Without honesty, what have we got in this life? Therefore, in the interest of honesty, when you think of Queenie, don't think of a thing. Think of . . . of . . . of a goddess! Yes, a goddess. I knew it would come to me. Thanks for your patience.

My hearing is very sharp, and in the quiet of the night it's at its sharpest. For example, from my place on the grandfather clock, I could hear that the inn was not quite fast asleep. From upstairs came a single soft footstep, a man's footstep. Did we have a man guest at the moment?

I don't pay attention to details like that. I know Mom's happier when we have guests, and Mom's happiness is important to me—within limits, of course—but I prefer no guests. If you're headed this way, look into other inns. I'm sure there must be some.

Meanwhile, other faint sounds rose from the basement. We have a large and complicated basement, some of it new, some very old. These faint sounds came from the old part, faint scurrying sounds, sneaky but very busy, sounds that could only be made by a mouse. All at once, even though I'd had a very full day, mostly curled up right here, I was no longer the slightest bit sleepy. I've been on many hunting trips in my life, day or night, good weather or bad, and never regretted a single one.

I glided down to the floor and became one with the night, just one of my many tricks. Arthur, as you may know already, has one trick and one trick only—playing dead. Playing dead or becoming one with the night: You be the judge.

There are several routes to the basement, one or two known only to me. I was headed for the kitchen, where the door to the back stairs never quite closes properly, when I heard a car coming up the road in front of our place. Not unusual, even late at night, especially in summer. I heard the soft crunch of gravel, meaning the car had turned into our circular driveway. It crunched to a stop, the engine

26

purring, as humans sometimes say about engines, a very annoying way to describe the sound made by a bunch of metal parts banging around. Also annoying was the fact that we had a car sitting outside our place for no apparent reason. This was the moment for the dog of a household to step up and bark an angry bark or two, sending that car on its way, but this household did not have that kind of dog. We had the kind of dog who was fast asleep, most likely in the family quarters, sprawled across Bro's bed, or Harmony's, or Mom's, shifting now and then to get more comfortable, but otherwise a log, more or less.

I turned and went back to the front hall. Through the tall, narrow window by the front door, I saw a car parked at the top of the circle, headlights off, but I see well at night, much better than you, and could make out a woman behind the wheel. She had short blond hair of the very pale kind, like the white of the moon, and wore lots of lipstick, which made her lips look coal black in the greenish light from her dashboard. She also wore glasses of the kind called cat's eye, a bit of a puzzle to me. Did humans who wore them think they were somehow catlike? Good luck with that.

I was considering making a mental list of all the things I do better than you, when I heard soft footsteps coming down the main stairs. I, already a shadow, moved in among the bigger shadows by the umbrella stand.

Down the stairs came a man, a shadowy sort of man. I couldn't make out his face, but his movements were . . . were actually somewhat catlike! That was a big surprise, especially since I'd just been thinking about this very thing. I'm not surprised very often, so whatever was going on couldn't be good.

The man crossed the hall, headed toward the door and therefore my way. A moonbeam angled through the narrow window and lit his face. Then came another surprise. This was an old man, with shaggy white eyebrows and wild white hair. An old man who moved like a much younger man, and not only that, but a catlike younger man? Was this the kind of guest we needed?

He went right by me—a stony look on his face, made stonier by the moonlight—opened the door, and went outside, leaving the door slightly ajar. Through that opening, I watched him walking toward the car. Was he leaving? That was my hope.

The driver's side window rolled down. The woman with the black lips and cat's-eye glasses spoke in a low, angry voice. "How could this have happened?"

"Sorry, babe," he said. "Not my fault."

The woman in the cat's-eye glasses glanced at the inn. "Keep your voice down." She stuck a small package out the window, about the size of one of the boxes fast-food burgers come in. The sight of those fast-food burger boxes brings out the worst in someone I'm sure I don't have to name.

The white-haired man took the package. The woman drove off. The man turned and started back toward the inn. I stepped toward the door, rested one of my front paws against it, and leaned in. The door swung shut, closing with a satisfying click. He was not the kind of guest we needed.

Now, where was I? Ah, yes, my little mousy pal, having some nice mousy playtime down in the basement. What a treat he had in store—a playmate appearing out of the blue, taking the trouble to keep him company! Who doesn't like a bit of company? I don't actually, but never mind that. Mice lead boring lives. How kind of me to liven things up for them!

I turned toward the kitchen, but hadn't taken a step before a commotion started up on the other side of the door. At first, a quiet commotion: some twisting of the knob, and then a "Huh?" A forceful kind of *huh*, not the sound you'd expect from an old guy, and neither would you expect those catlike movements. Humans can be very puzzling when you stop to think about it. But why waste your time? I took another step toward the kitchen, but the human on the other side of the door didn't seem to be going away.

"What the—?!" he said. And "Can you believe this?"

What was so hard to understand? It was time for this guy to get in his car and drive off, preferably to somewhere far away. Wasn't China far away? I remembered hearing that. Drive off to China! Go on! Scat!

But this bothersome—what to call him? A former guest? That sounded right. This bothersome former guest showed no sign of driving off to China. Instead he did some rattling of the doorknob, followed by "Hey! Open up!" and then a knock-knock KNOCK-KNOCK, followed by what might have been a kick.

"Ouch!" he said.

Yes, a kick for sure. Finally he thought to press the little button beside the door. That made the chimes chime, a sound I'm not fond of. I drew back behind the umbrella stand.

Footsteps sounded on the back stairs that led up to the family quarters. Bare feet, light-stepping, and sure-footed, Mom. She came into the hall, turned on a light, went to the door. The chimes chimed again.

Mom called through the door. "Who is it?"

"Me!" said the man.

One of Mom's eyes narrowed slightly. That would not be a good look on most people, but it didn't take anything away from Mom's beauty, only showed how supersmart she was, as well as beautiful. Was there a smarter human out there? Well, the twins' pal Maxie Millipat was supposed to be very smart. The last time I'd seen him—at the village green on kite day—he'd gotten tangled up in his own kite, a kite shaped like a huge rat, by the way, and gotten lifted right off the ground. So my money's still on Mom in the smart department. I actually have no money, but also don't need it. My eyes are like glittering gold coins, as people often remarked.

Meanwhile Mom was saying, "Do I know you? I don't recognize your voice."

Then came a surprise. When the man answered, his voice had changed, turning feeble and scratchy—although my ears could still hear the real voice underneath, if you get what I mean. And if you don't, well, too bad.

"Norman Ware, of course," he said. "From the . . . the Daffy Duck Room or whatever you call it."

Mom opened the door. "Why, Mr. Ware, didn't you say you were in for the night? Otherwise I'd have given you the key."

"Why all these stupid rules?" said Mr. Ware, pushing past Mom and entering the hall.

Mom closed the door and gazed at Mr. Ware, who was now on his way up the stairs. "It's the Daffodil Room," she said, her voice like ice. Could I somehow meow in an icy way? I looked forward to giving it a try.

Mr. Ware did not answer, just went up the stairs and out of sight. Mom's gaze followed him until he was gone.

Then she headed into the small parlor, which led to the back stairs and the family quarters. I went the other way, through the kitchen and down the basement stairs.

Hunting mice—well, not hunting, let's just call it playing with my little buddies—is one of those hobbies that never gets old. For one thing, there are always new mice to meet. You may be thinking, what happens to the old ones? Perhaps I'll have a chance to get to that a little later.

The basement at the Blackberry Hill Inn is very big and has two parts. There's the newer part with the furnace room, storeroom, sports equipment room, laundry room, broken-furniture room, and wine cellar with no wine in it, and there's the old cellar, with a dirt floor, lots of cobwebs, and rusted farm equipment from long ago. Way back in one corner stands the huge old boiler, which had heated the whole house at one time, Mom said, but now just walled off a little space where mice would feel safe. They never learn, which is the most important fact to know about mice.

I made my way around to the back of the old boiler. Everything was shadowy. Did the mice think I was just another shadow? That would be a typical micey thought, the kind of thought they would cling to until it was too late. And now came a micey smell, not so different from the smell of peanuts, but dustier and with a hint of squirrel. I moved toward the smell, so silently I couldn't even hear myself. Hunting-type things were happening, but slowly, which was often the case at first. I heard the scritch-scritch of mouse paws up to something, followed by a faint lippy sort of sound that meant my soon-to-be mouse buddy had found something to nibble on. I glided closer, and then through the small coal chute window high in the wall, where coal had been delivered in the old days, came a silvery moonbeam.

I saw my mouse, a surprisingly fat specimen, sitting up and munching on some sort of crumbs. At the same moment, my mouse saw me. A surprisingly fat mouse, but also surprisingly quick. In no time at all, he'd scrambled straight up the wall, leaped onto the coal chute, and was darting toward the small window where . . . where there was still a hole in one of the windowpanes! Hadn't Elrod fixed that hole yet? What was a handyman for? How would I go about getting him fired?

But that thought was for the future. Right now my little playmate was shooting through the hole in the window-pane and out into the night. I sprang onto the coal chute, squeezed through the hole, and followed.

And there he was, tiny legs churning as fast as they could, although he was actually advancing quite slowly— not yet even halfway across the side lawn, which led to the woods and the possibility of many hidey-holes and a lot of tedious work for me. You can be quick without being fast—an interesting fact about mice. I'm both, as I'm sure you already know.

I ran after my fattish friend, not my fastest, since the outcome was not in doubt, more of a lope. I'm not much of a TV watcher, but once I'd caught a show about tigers. Their lope is something like mine—on a bigger scale, no doubt, if not quite as graceful, which I mention merely to keep you in the picture.

Loping along on a moonlit night, one bound or two from the prey—well, let's not put it that way—how about a teammate in a game he didn't yet know we were playing: Life was good. I took one last lope, then bounded, launching myself into the night air.

Normally not much happens in these midair moments, except a lovely feeling of good cheer coming over me. But this time things were different. First, my little teammate turned his little head and saw me. That was unusual, since my movements are silent, especially in midair. Around then was when I heard a strange sound from above. It reminded me of the fwap-fwap the ceiling fan in the Big Room made before Elrod fixed it. Well, not fixed, since the ceiling fan ended up in pieces in the storage shed. But at least we no longer had to deal with the annoying fwap-fwap.

I only mention the ceiling fan to give you an idea of the sound coming from above. My mousy pal's gaze rose up in that direction and I saw terror in his eyes. Very satisfying, of course, but then came a big surprise, quite close to a real shock. It turned out that the mouse wasn't afraid of me! Well, I'm sure he was, but that fear was being dwarfed by another one. An instant later a huge white owl swooped down—right before my eyes—and snatched up the mouse in its enormous claws, fwap-fwapping back up into the night sky.

I'm a hunter of birds, but small ones. Cardinals, finches, robins, that sort of thing. Certainly not owls. I'd seen owls, always in daytime. Once Harmony had pointed to one, sleeping on a high branch and looking peaceful. "Watch out for owls, Queenie," she'd said. I don't pay much attention to what humans say, but I make an exception for Harmony.

The next thing I knew, I was scrambling up the vine-covered trellis on the near side of the inn, leaping from there onto a second-floor balcony, almost . . . almost like . . . like I'd had a fright. And even . . . even panicked, the slightest bit.

But no! Impossible! Queenie does not have frights, and would never panic. Or scramble! Good grief, what an awful idea! Me? Scrambling? I got a grip. Then I hissed, a hiss that said, "I am Queenie, large and in charge." Except for the large part. The point was I'd regained my composure, if in fact I'd ever lost it, and who would believe that? Not me, my friends.

The balcony led to a sliding door, partly open on

a summer night. Beyond the slider was one of the guest rooms, the walls yellow. Yellow walls meant the Daffodil Room. I peered in.

Mr. Ware sat at the makeup table. He opened the package the woman in the car had given him and took out a small green ball.

"Green?" he said. "What's the matter with her?"

He gazed at the green ball with distaste, and then stuck it on the end of his nose. Humans could surprise you, almost never in a good way. Now we had a series of unpleasant surprises. First, Mr. Ware pulled off his wild white hair—a wig, I believe, is the name—and then tugged off one of his shaggy white eyebrows. He was raising his hand toward the other eyebrow when he caught sight of me. For a moment he looked alarmed, but then his expression changed.

"Well well," he said, with no trace now of the old man voice. "You're still quite the beauty, aren't you?"

True, but somehow, coming from him, it didn't please me.

"Maybe more so than ever," Mr. Ware added, which didn't quite make sense to me. "Come on in. Why don't we get to know each other a bit. Maybe I could scare up a treat of some sort."

I gazed at him: a dark-haired guy with a thin brown eyebrow and a shaggy white one, also wearing a green ball on his nose. Had he been a guest here before? I thought so, but that didn't mean I wanted to get to know him. I slipped between the balcony railings, pitter-pattered down the trellis, came down on the lawn.

Then, from high above: Hoot! Hoot! Hoot!

A big, empty flowerpot lay on its side in the strip of garden by the house. I stepped into it and curled up.

FIVE

ARTHUR

WAKEE-WAKEE, ARTHUR. IT'S THE big day!"

I opened my eyes, found that I was in Bro's bedroom, lying comfortably on his pillow. Bro himself seemed to be already up and about, in fact standing over me, fully dressed and with that green Frisbee in his hand. Oh, no. The green Frisbee? Not again! I wriggled deeper into the pillow and closed my eyes.

"C'mon, Arthur. Last chance for a little practice. Mr. Salming says practice makes perfect."

Mr. Salming? The baseball and hockey coach, also the mailman? What could he have meant by practice makes perfect? Did mail carriers practice delivering the mail? I had no idea, and realized right away I'd come to a dead end. I'm fine with dead ends. I rolled over, had a nice stretch, made some sort of sighing sound—no idea why—and dropped down into dreamland.

"Arthur! Step it up! You've had enough sleep. Let's move!"

What was this? Bro still around? Didn't he have chores

to do? As for sleep, how did you know if you'd had enough? The answer came to me: You only knew if you'd had enough sleep if you couldn't get back to sleep! Wow! My own mind had figured that out? Was this the start of something big? Was I going to be brilliant from here on in? Suddenly I sprang out of bed! Maybe not actually springing, but I did sort of tumble down onto the floor.

"Hey! Arthur! Good boy!" Bro had a big smile on his face. I'd . . . I'd pleased him! That was nice. I wondered how. If only I knew, I could do it again. I followed him downstairs and onto the lawn, tail held high. I felt strong, fast, smart—like a million bucks! Whatever those were.

"Okay, one last time," Bro said, and he scaled the green Frisbee into the air.

One last time until what? I was a bit confused.

"Go, Arthur, go!"

I ran back into the house. When Bro says go, I go. Who's a good good boy?

"Oh, Arthur!" he said. Or something like that. I couldn't be sure on account of this commotion that seemed to be happening, commotion involving me and Bertha. Have I mentioned Bertha yet? She's the cook. Since we only serve breakfast here at the inn, Bertha's only around in the mornings. It took me quite some time to put that together, but I'm pretty sure I've got it now. And here's something really amazing: If Bertha's around then it must be morning! I know what you're thinking: Wow, that Arthur! Am I right?

Bertha's a big strong woman of the no-nonsense kind. She has a boyfriend named Big Fred. He's the boss of the volunteer fire department, bigger and stronger than just about anybody, although Bertha calls him Freddie, like he's a little kid. The reason I mention Big Fred is that I spotted him in the background, munching on a slice of sausage. I recognized the smell right away. Big Fred's a fan of a certain kind of sausage with a yellow label, a kind that I'm a big fan of, too. And what was that sticking out of his chest pocket? It sure looked to me like the top of a package with a yellow label.

Spotting Big Fred was what led to all the commotion, because I took my eye off where I was going, which happened to be straight into Bertha. Somehow I got all tangled up in her apron, and untangling me, she got tangled up in it, too, and maybe even started to lose her balance. But Big Fred was suddenly right there to catch her, one arm around her waist. He even caught me! By the scruff of the neck, as it turned out, and not the waist, maybe not possible in my case, since there was a chance I didn't have a waist. Meanwhile, Big Fred and Bertha were exchanging an interesting sort of look.

"Thanks, Freddie," she said.

"Any time," said Big Fred.

Bertha laughed.

"And what's with you, my friend?" Big Fred said, putting me down. "Never seen you move so fast."

"He's actually not getting with the program this morning," Bertha said.

"What program?" said Big Fred.

Bertha pointed out the doorway. Bro was standing in the yard, the Frisbee at his feet. Bro's head was down and he looked kind of . . . unhappy. Were programs something on TV? Was I supposed to be on TV? Only one way to find out: I headed for the Big Room, where a TV hung on the wall in one corner. Wow! I'd solved a problem, and all by myself.

From behind, I heard Big Fred say, "Hey, Bro, come over here for a sec. And bring that Frisbee."

The moment I entered the Big Room, I sniffed a nice surprise in the air. You can't see air, but all sorts of things are going on in it all the time. For example, here in the Big Room we had what you might call a tiny stream of Cheez-It aroma flowing right up to the tip of my nose. It was a snap to follow the stream to its source, which was under the red leather chair near the fireplace, where I'd had successful fishing expeditions in the past.

I got down on my belly and wriggled my way under the red leather chair. And there, next to one of the chair's feet—a claw-foot, I believe they're called, somewhat threatening in appearance—I found a lovely Cheez-It, a bit dusty but otherwise undamaged. I snapped it up.

After that, I lingered under the chair for a while, licking my muzzle and . . . what was the expression? Enjoying the day? That was it. I licked my muzzle and enjoyed the day until it suddenly struck me that I'd come to the Big Room for some reason other than finding a Cheez-It. What could that reason have been? I searched my mind. It happened to be rather empty at the moment, so the search was nice and quick. I turned up nothing.

Therefore I'd come to a dead end. When you come to a dead end—and I'm sure you know this already—there's only one thing to do, namely give yourself a real good shake. Get those ears flapping around, whap whap whap, upside the head. That'll clear your mind, and pronto!

With just about the clearest mind I'd ever had in my whole life, I trotted out of the Big Room. Down the hall, Big Fred was handing Bro the green Frisbee, now wrapped in a plastic bag.

"Keep it in the bag," Big Fred said.

"Why?" said Bro.

"Gave it some mojo," Big Fred told him. "Wouldn't want to waste it."

"Arthur! Watch where you're going!"

Uh-oh. On my way out of the Big Room, had I come

close to tripping up Harmony, who seemed to be headed toward the front door with Queenie in her arms? Yikes! There was even a chance it was my fault. I followed them, my mind fixed on making things better, possibly by licking Harmony's foot, or something of that nature. I inched closer, stuck out my tongue, and—and Queenie, suddenly popping up on Harmony's shoulder, her golden eyes on fire in a way I never like to see, hissed in my direction. Actually right at me, a hiss that's very hard to describe. But it makes my hair stand on end. And her hair stands on end when she does it! Which is a very scary sight. Mix that in with the scary sound of the hiss, and . . . and I dropped way back. The foot licking would have to wait for another time.

I dropped way back, but not entirely out of the picture. Hard to explain why, but it had something to do with Queenie being carried. Arthur likes being carried, too! Were folks somehow missing that? How could I help them understand?

Soon we were on the side lawn, me at a safe distance. No sign now of Bertha or Big Fred, but Bro was still there, now looking much more chipper. He stuck the green Frisbee in his backpack and was hoisting it on his back when Harmony said, "Hey, Bro—help me give Queenie a bath."

"She hates water," said Bro.

"Which is why I need your help," Harmony said.

"She keeps herself pretty clean, like on her own."

43

"Bro! It's a beauty contest!"

A beauty contest? Was I in it? If Queenie was, then I had to be, too. That was only fair. We play hard in this family but we play fair. "When you cheat, you're cheating yourself most of all." That was something Mom said. I think it's about being fair, but if I'm wrong, skip this part.

Meanwhile we were all headed toward the pond—not the Lilypad Pond near the patio, where guests often had a cool drink at the end of the day, but the big pond beyond the old barn, where we sometimes went for a swim, me and the twins, the twins swimming and me steering them back to shore. They love when I do that! Even if they pretend not to. What characters they can be sometimes!

Soon we were all down by the pond. Harmony, still carrying Queenie, kicked off her flip-flops and waded in up to her knees. Queenie didn't move a muscle, but the hot look in her eyes heated up even more.

"Remember her last bath?" Bro said.

"This will be different," said Harmony. "I've done some research. First we make Queenie feel totally at ease."

"How?"

"By stroking her gently and saying nice things." Harmony began stroking Queenie's back. "Nice Queenie," she said. "Who's the nicest cat in the whole wide world?" She turned to Bro. "Now you."

"Now me what?"

"Stroke her. Say nice things."

Bro kicked off his flip-flops and stepped into the pond. He reached out and stroked Queenie. "Nice Queenie," he said. "Who's the nicest cat in the whole pond?"

"Bro!"

"As well as the whole wide world."

Soon they were both stroking Queenie and both saying nice things. Was Queenie paying attention? I had no idea, but her eyes were burning. By now I'd forgotten—if I'd ever known—the point of all this. But is it all right to point out that Arthur likes getting stroked? That Arthur likes hearing nice things about him?

"Okay," Harmony said. "She seems pretty calm. There's shampoo in my back pocket. Take it out and be ready. I'm going to lower her very slowly in the water, and when she's used to it you pour a little shampoo on her and rub it in gently."

Bro reached into Harmony's back pocket, took out the shampoo bottle, and flipped it to his other hand. Bro flips a lot of things that way—pencils, soda cans, and of course balls of many types. Mr. Salming says Bro has soft hands, which are what you want for catching, and I'm sure Bro would have caught the shampoo bottle if events hadn't taken a sudden turn.

Did I play a role in this sudden turn? Kind of. Bertha says the mind does tricks on you. I myself know one trick, namely playing dead, and maybe that's what I should have done at that moment, out there by the pond. But the sight of that shampoo bottle spinning in the air made me realize—finally realize!—that Bro very badly wanted me to fetch. I love Bro and want to make him happy. There! Now you have the whole story. Do I really need to describe what happened next, a whole busy chain of activity?

I don't see why, but in case I'm wrong, I suppose we should start with me springing out over the water and snatching that shampoo bottle right out of midair, like the great athlete I am, deep deep inside. Except that part—the snatching out of midair—didn't actually happen. But I did make contact with the shampoo bottle, don't doubt that, not for a second. The only problem was it bounced off my muzzle and spun even higher in the air. At that point I did something pretty amazing, even surprising myself. Somehow I managed to twist around—how was I staying aloft for so long? Wow, just wow!—and snapped once more at the bottle. Which I didn't quite touch this time. Still, no harm, no foul, not at this point. The real difficulty began on my way down, when I sort of hurtled into Harmony and knocked a certain beauty contestant clear out of her arms and into the pond.

An instant later—KER-SPLASH! I hit the water myself, went down and down, and there on the muddy bottom, glinting in a ray of sunshine, lay the shampoo bottle! I grabbed it and headed up. Who's a good good boy?

46

I shot through the surface of the pond—or at least got to it. Things had changed up there. First, some strange white stringy-looking thing was swimming away and making a horrible shrieking noise. Harmony and Bro seemed to be swimming after the stringy thing, at the same time shouting at each other in a way that didn't seem brotherly or sisterly. In short, this was not so easy to understand. I climbed up on shore, dropped the shampoo bottle at the feet of nobody, and gave myself a real good shake.

Nothing like a good shake for clearing the head. And what a lot of stuff I had in my head to get rid of! This had been such a busy day already, and it seemed to be getting busier. The strange stringy thing scrambled out of the pond and . . . and started giving itself a good shake! That was a bit of a surprise, and then came a bigger one. The strange stringy thing got all fluffed out and turned out to be Queenie! And in a real bad mood. She opened her mouth wide, exposing those alarmingly long teeth—long and very sharp, as I knew for sure, unfortunately—and let out a kind of scream that seemed to stop the whole day in its tracks. Then she took off for the woods, like a white streak across the meadow. I had to remind myself that I, Arthur, was much faster.

I was standing there by the pond, reminding myself of my awesome speed, when I noticed someone coming across the meadow, namely the old man with the wild white hair, Mr. Ware if I was remembering right. Whoa! Had I seen him without that wild white hair? I was trying to get Mr. Ware all sorted out in my mind when Harmony and Bro came charging out of the water.

"Queenie! Queenie!"

Queenie paid no attention. She raced toward the woods. At that moment, Mr. Ware saw her just about to disappear among the trees. Mr. Ware stopped dead, a look of alarm on his face. Then he opened his mouth and spoke in a clear but not loud voice. All he said was, "Meow."

Queenie slammed on the brakes. Then she turned, walked straight to Mr. Ware, and sat at his feet. He smiled a very small smile.

The twins ran up. "Oh, thank you, Mr. . . . Mr. . . ." Harmony said.

"Ware," said Mr. Ware.

"Hey," said Bro. "How did you do that?"

"I speak cat," Mr. Ware told him.

I'd been trying to make up my mind about Mr. Ware. But now I knew. He was scary, and that was that.

SIX

QUEENIE

IN THOSE MOMENTS DOWN AT THE pond—and not just at the pond, but in it! The horror! Cast into the water, my whole body! Even my head, dunked right under. I was totally immersed in water! All of me! Has anything worse happened to anyone ever?

I know what you're saying: But just think, Queenie. You're a hero. True, of course, and deservedly so, but did I ask to be a hero? No. What is the one thing I ask for in this life? To be alone! I want to be alone. Is that so hard to understand? Why does everyone clamor to be around me 24-7? The answer to that question is what came to me in those moments down at—and in!—the pond. Everyone is drawn to me on account of my beauty. My beauty ends up being a curse as well as a blessing.

Oh, the horror!

And in the midst of all the horror, our bedraggled—yes, bedraggled—little hero, on her way to a life of complete aloneness in the deepest, darkest corner of the deep, dark woods, suddenly hears a sympathetic voice, a sympathetic voice calling out in her own language.

"Meow!"

Meow. A beautiful sound, perfectly spoken. It cut through all the badness. I turned in the direction of that perfect sound and before I knew it, I seemed to be at the feet of that strange man, Mr. Ware, the one who sometimes looked old and sometimes looked young.

Right now, he looked old. Did I like this man, old or young? I did not. Plus, I was soaking wet! And probably not looking my best, not even close. Who am I if I'm not looking my best? I faced that terrible question for the first time in my life, and began digging my claws into Mr. Ware's shoe. He gazed calmly down at me and said, "Meow."

This time he said it in a way that was even nicer than the time before, a perfect, lovely cat sound coming from the mouth of this human. I forgot all about what I'd been planning to do with my claws, and instead went absolutely still. Mr. Ware bent down and began fluffing out my fur, which was exactly what I wanted.

The twins came over. "Wow, Mr. Ware," Harmony said. "You're so good with cats."

Mr. Ware said nothing. He stepped back and Harmony picked me up.

"How come?" Bro said.

Mr. Ware raised one of his shaggy white eyebrows. Not a real eyebrow; I knew that but no longer cared.

"I mean how come you're so good with cats?" Bro said.

Mr. Ware spoke in his scratchy old man voice. Not his real voice, but I no longer cared about that, either. "Their attitude mirrors my own."

"Meaning you're like a cat?" Bro said.

"Meaning just what I said," said Mr. Ware. "No more, no less."

Bro gets this look on his face when he's not going to let something go. He had it now, but before he could speak, Harmony said, "Thank you for helping Queenie. We were trying to get her ready for the beauty contest at the county fair, but I'm not sure we'd have made it without you."

"Hey," said Bro. "Do you want to come?"

"I have no interest in county fairs," Mr. Ware said.

There are times when I fall into a sort of trance. If Mom notices me in one, she says, "Queenie's having deep thoughts again."

Mom is Mom, of course, and more often right about things than any human I'd ever met, but she was wrong about deep thoughts. The truth is that in my trances I have no thoughts at all. What I have in my trances are feelings. Actually just a single feeling, the same one every time. It's a feeling of being huge while everything around me is tiny. A lovely feeling, which you probably have never experienced and never will.

The reason I bring this up is that as Mr. Ware walked

away from us, headed back across the meadow to the inn, I fell into one of my trances. When I snapped out of it we were no longer in the meadow, but walking down Harvest Road. I'd been on Harvest Road several times, but only on nighttime excursions, somewhat secret excursions that might have been all about hunting, a fact I'll keep to myself.

In the direction I always went, Harvest Road ended at the village green, a popular nighttime spot for all sorts of little critters. But we were going in the other direction, me in the special backpack with the see-through mesh, a backpack Harmony wears in front when I'm in it. Queenie rides in front, as I made clear the first day the backpack appeared at the Blackberry Hill Inn. When dealing with humans, you want to establish the rules right out of the gate.

Next to us we had Bro, carrying the green Frisbee, and a certain other party, sniffing at every spot where one of his kind had stopped to pee, which turned out to be many. In this direction, Harvest Road led past a farm, some woods, another farm, and then came a very big unpaved parking lot with lots of cars and pickups already there, and then beyond that a whole big and noisy scene, hard to take in all at once even if you wanted to, which I did not.

"Ferris wheel!" said Harmony.

"Bumper cars!" said Bro.

And on and on like that. We crossed the parking lot and came to the ticket booth.

"Two kids under sixteen?" said the gum-chewing woman in the booth. "Ten bucks. No charge for the cat, especially one this beautiful."

I liked this gum-chewing woman immediately. She had long hair, wore lots of jewelry, and had a look on her face like she was about to smile any second.

Meanwhile Bro was reaching into his pocket and coming up empty, as usual. "Harm? I'll pay you back."

"If I live to be a million," said Harmony.

The gun-chewing woman laughed. Harmony handed over some money.

"Know about the beauty contest?" the woman said.

"That's why we're here," said Harmony.

"Thought so," said the woman.

"And for the Frisbee contest," Bro said.

The woman's eyes shifted to Arthur, at that moment scratching vigorously behind his ear. "Hmmf," she said.

We entered the fairgrounds. Ferris wheel, check. Bumper cars, check. The reek of cotton candy in the air, check. Noise, check. Crowds, check. Bro's mouth hung open, and so did Harmony's, if only a little. After what seemed like several days, we reached a booth selling something that didn't smell very appetizing to me.

"Corn dogs!" yelled the man in the booth. "Corn dogs heah!"

Around then was when Arthur got put on a leash. Being

leashed was unthinkable to me, but Arthur didn't seem to mind or even notice. He just kept ambling along, sniff-sniff-sniffing all the way. That was irritating. What was wrong with him? Why didn't he mind? Why didn't he notice?

Also irritating was the summer heat, the dust in the air, plus the smells of farm animals, many animals of many kinds, wafting our way from one of the big tents at the far end of the fairgrounds. When and where was the beauty contest? It was time to win this thing and get out of here.

But no. We hadn't even gotten past the corn dog booth when a clown stepped in front of our path. I'd seen a clown once before at Emma's birthday party, Emma being one of Harmony's pals. I hadn't liked that one and I didn't like this one—a tall man—the man smell very clear even in this hot, dusty, greasy air—wearing enormous floppy shoes, one green, one yellow, a striped and polka-dotted clown suit, and a big red ball on the end of his nose.

"Well well," he said in a voice that I might have considered warm and friendly if I hadn't decided to dislike the guy, "welcome to the fair, you two lovely things. And to your humans as well!"

"Ha-ha," said Bro.

"Ha," said Harmony. I gazed into the distance. Arthur hid behind Bro's leg.

"Hey, little fella," said the clown, "have no fear!" He reached down to pat Arthur, then pretended to get all caught up in the leash, tilting sideways one way, all rubbery, then the other way, crying, "Woo woo, woo, woo," like he was out of his mind with fear, and the twins started laughing, and a crowd formed around us—a crowd within the crowd, if you see what I mean, absolutely dreadful—and I stuck my claws through the mesh, where there was nothing to claw but air. I didn't care for clowns, not at all. And especially this one, with the boozy breath. Boozy breath often leads to problems down the road—one of the first things you learn in the hospitality industry, which is our industry, of course, at the Blackberry Hill Inn.

After way too long, something else caught the clown's attention, possibly something having to do with a giant blob of cotton candy. The cotton candy smell reminded me of something, but was I capable of concentrating my mind at the moment? No, not even I. The crowd flowed away, following the pink blob. And there, right in front of us, stood Maxie Millipat.

"Yo, dudes," he said.

"Knock it off," Harmony told him.

"My lingo too cool for ya?" said Maxie. "You jelly of me?"

Maxie was a scrawny kid, possibly a genius, according to the *Green Mountain Record*, where there'd been an article not long ago about Maxie and something he was building in his backyard to attract beings from space. That hadn't interested me in the slightest, but I'd loved the look on Mom's face as she read the article aloud at the kitchen table.

"Do you even want to be cool, Maxie?" Harmony said.

"What I want," said Maxie, one of his legs now twitching, "is to set up a booth right here at the fair and get people to pay to guess my IQ. And here's the kicker! The prize will be a stuffed Einstein doll!"

"You know your IQ?" Harmony said.

"Of course," said Maxie. "My mom took me to Boston and I got tested."

"Why?" said Bro.

"Huh?" Maxie said.

"Why'd you want to get your IQ tested?"

Maxie opened his mouth, closed it, opened it again, but no sound came out.

"Maybe if it was a little higher, you'd know the answer," Bro said.

Maxie's face turned pink. "It is high! Really high! Go on—guess."

"Nine hundred," Bro said.

"Hmm," said Maxie. "Not that high. IQs don't go to nine hundred."

"Why not?" said Bro.

Maxie's face got pinker. He turned to Harmony. "Explain to him."

"Explain what?"

"IQ."

"What about it?"

"Why you should get it tested," Maxie said.

Harmony thought. Through the backpack I could feel her heartbeat, boom-boom, boom-boom, nice and steady. "To give your parents a thrill," she said.

Maxie's eyes shifted, like something going on in his head had grabbed his attention. Then he gave his head a little shake—like to chase away whatever it was—and he said, "Tell you what—I'll show you where I got the idea."

"What idea?" said Harmony.

"For the IQ booth. It's still a good idea—I'll just have to iron out the bugs, that's all."

"When the bugs are gone, there'll be nothing left," Bro said.

Harmony glanced at him in surprise.

We followed Maxie past a stall where people were throwing darts at balloons hanging on a back wall, balloons shaped like various creatures, including . . . including a cat?

Pop!

"And we have another winner! Pick out your prize, little lady!"

Oh, how horrible! Why was I here? And then I remembered: the beauty contest. Sometimes in life you've just got to suck it up. I sucked it up.

We came to another booth. This one was better. No darts, no cat-shaped balloon, no balloons of any kind. All it had were some teddy bears on a pole—not unlike the teddy bear Harmony once had, before Arthur did what he did—plus a scale like the one in Mom's bathroom, except with a pole sticking up from it, and on top of the pole a round clocklike thing that reminded me of my grandfather clock. A girl stood beside the scale. She was maybe Harmony's age, but not big and strong like Harmony, much skinnier, with pale skin and huge dark eyes, and thick long braids that hung down her back. She also wore a sparkling gown and a sparkling crown. I like sparkles so I liked her. Life can be so simple.

"Step right up," she said, waving a sparkling wand, her voice on the small side, although somehow very clear. "I, Magical Miranda, will guess your weight to within one pound or you win a teddy bear."

"Watch this," Maxie whispered.

Magical Miranda's huge eyes shifted in his direction, showed nothing, and shifted back. Meanwhile a big bearded guy had stepped right up.

"What's it cost?" he said.

"Three dollars," said Magical Miranda.

The big bearded guy handed over some money, which she tucked away. She held out the sparkling wand, close to the big bearded guy, but not touching him. Then, without studying him—or really looking closely at all—she said, "Two hundred and forty-five pounds."

The man's eyebrows rose.

"Please get on the scale," Magical Miranda said.

The man got on the scale. The needle on the round clock-like thing started moving and stopped with a little ding.

"Would you read the number, please?" said Magical Miranda.

"Two forty-five," the man said.

"Thank you, sir. Who's next? I, Magical Miranda, will guess your weight to within one pound or you win a teddy bear."

By now a small crowd was forming. Another big bearded guy—we seem to have lots of them in these parts—stepped forward. He looked to be about the same size and shape as the first big bearded guy, a beefy-type shape, I believe it's called, and was dressed like him, too—shorts, T-shirt, dusty work boots—but this one had a different expression on his face, an expression that reminded me of foxes. I once had a surprise late-evening encounter with a fox, a real-life nightmare best forgotten.

The fox-like big guy gave Magical Miranda the money. Again, she held the sparkling wand close to him and without spending any time at all, and in that small but clear voice, she said, "Two hundred nineteen pounds."

"Huh?" said the fox-like big guy.

Magical Miranda didn't answer, but simply motioned to the scale. The man stepped on. The needle moved and stopped. Ding.

"Would you read the number, please?"

"Two . . . nineteen," said the man.

The man shook his head, walked away, happened to bump into the other big bearded guy.

"That's all you weigh?" said big bearded guy number one. "Two nineteen?"

"I got real light bones," said big bearded guy number two. "But how did she know?"

They both eyed Miranda. She was saying, "Who's next? I, Magical Miranda, will guess your weight to within one pound or you win a teddy bear."

Maxie stepped forward. "Do you do dogs?" he said.

"I've never done a dog," said Magical Miranda. "Do you mean this one?" She looked down at Arthur, now lying on his side in the dirt, eyes closed.

"Yeah," said Maxie. "This one."

Magical Miranda gazed at Arthur with her huge dark eyes. "Why not?" she said.

SEVEN

ARTHUR

I LAY IN THE DIRT AT THIS FAIR OR WHAT-
ever it was, dirt that felt soft and comfortable, maybe
the most comfortable dirt I'd ever lain in. Above me
some sort of conversation was going on.

"Well, Maxie," Bro was saying, "it's not your call."

"Not getting you, Bro my friend," said Maxie.

"Arthur's not your dog," said Harmony.

I opened one eye.

"Meaning it's your call?" said Maxie.

Harmony nodded.

"But what about Arthur?" Maxie said. "Why isn't it
his call?"

Then they were all gazing down at me—Harmony, Bro,
Maxie, and the girl with huge dark eyes, possibly called
Magical Miranda, a fact I might have learned when I was
still on my feet. And all of them seemed to be interested
in me! Except for Queenie, in her mesh backpack, who
was looking at nothing, but in an annoyed sort of way. Was
something or other my call? I waited to find out more.

61

"Good point," Bro said. He crouched down. "Arthur? Want to step on the scale?"

Scale? I knew scale from the vet. You stepped on it and then she gave you a treat. I sniffed no treats but I rose anyway, being the hopeful type. Bro unclipped my leash. Why? I had no idea, but all in all I preferred no leash to leash.

"Hey," said a bystander—there seemed to be a bit of a crowd around us. "What a smart dog!"

I checked things out, saw no other dog but me. That had to mean something, and with a little more time I could have figured it out. Meanwhile where was the vet? Was Magical Miranda the vet? Her huge dark eyes were peering deep into mine.

"Arthur," she said. Magical Miranda's voice, not at all loud, sounded very clear, like she was right inside my head. "That's a nice name. Are you named after King Arthur?"

King Arthur? A new one on me, but I liked the sound of it.

"Actually," Harmony said, "he's named after the FedEx guy. He's the one who told us there were puppies available at a farm down the road."

"Even better in a way," said Magical Miranda.

Harmony has a way of giving people a quick glance from time to time, although I have no clue what it means. She gave Miranda one of those quick glances now. Miranda noticed and smiled a small smile. Then her face went back to normal. I realized her normal face didn't look happy.

"All of this is pretty interesting," Maxie said. "Not. Now tell us your guess. What does Arthur weigh?"

Miranda's huge dark eyes shifted in Maxie's direction. "Three dollars," she said.

"Ha-ha," said Maxie. "That's a good one. But as everyone's been saying, he's not my pooch."

"But you're the one who brought up the whole—" Bro began. He stopped when Harmony gave him the tiniest head shake, hardly any movement at all. She dug some money out of her pocket and gave it to Miranda.

Miranda tucked the money away. She pointed this sort of sparkly stick at me. Oh, no. Was she about to throw the stick and start up a game of fetch? You have to be in a special mood for fetch—a very special mood—and I was not.

But Miranda didn't throw the stick. Instead she gave it a little wave and said, "Seventy-eight pounds."

"No way," Bro said.

"No?" said Miranda.

"Harm? What did he weigh at the vet?"

"Sixty-five," said Harmony. "Which the vet said was too much so he's been on a diet ever since."

I was on a diet? And no one told me? That didn't seem fair.

"Care to change your guess?" said Maxie.

The huge dark eyes stayed on him.

"Like," Maxie explained, "to some other number? Maybe a bit lower?"

"Arthur," said Miranda, not looking at me but still watching Maxie, "step on the scale."

Scale? I didn't see any scale. A scale was just a metal square in the floor with paper paw prints on it, and I didn't see anything like that. I got kind of confused, wandered around a bit, came to a kind of pole holding up a big round thing that reminded me of the grandfather clock in the front hall back home. When I see poles—telephone or parking meter poles, for example—I often give them a quick squirt, just to let everybody know ol' Arthur had passed by. Was marking this pole a good idea? I sat down to think about that.

"Whoa!" said Bro. "He went to the scale and sat right down, all by himself!"

Was he talking about me? How nice! I decided right then to mark the pole the first chance I got.

"What a good boy you are, Arthur!" said Miranda. She turned to Maxie. "You're Maxie?" she said.

"The one and only," said Maxie.

"If you please, the one and only Maxie, read the number on the scale."

Maxie checked the big round thing. "Seventy-seven and

nine-tenths, I'd say, possibly not quite even that, more like seventy-seven and three-quar—"

"Maxie!" said Harmony.

"Wow!" said someone in the crowd. There was even a bit of applause. They liked me here at this fair, or whatever it was. I was thinking about rolling over and playing dead—they'd go crazy—but before I could, people pushed forward toward Magical Miranda with money in their hands, and we—meaning me, Harmony, Bro, and Maxie, plus I suppose I have to mention Queenie—ended up back outside the stall. Leaving the pole unmarked! I decided to be cool about that. There's only so much you can do in this life.

"She's amazing!" Harmony said.

"You believe she's on the up and up?" said Maxie. "It's fixed."

"How?" said Bro.

"I'll figure it out," Maxie said.

Across the way, over by a popcorn stand, the clown was watching us. He smiled a huge red-lipped smile. At first, I thought he was the clown who'd gotten tangled up in my leash, an unpleasant moment for me. Then I noticed his nose was green, not red, so it had to be some other clown. I wagged my tail.

"Ha-ha!" said the green-nosed clown.

A voice came from above. "Attention, all cats! Will

contestants in the first All-County Feline Beauty Contest please proceed to the main tent. The contest begins in thirty minutes."

Cat beauty contest? Didn't sound very interesting to me. There was a barbecue smell in the air. Why not follow that smell and see where it led? I saw no reason not to, took a few steps in the right direction, and . . . and got clipped back onto the leash.

EIGHT

QUEENIE

SO THE UPSHOT OF ALL THIS WAS
that Arthur weighed too much? Some of us start
out already knowing what others are seeking.
Need I say more? Now, after way too long, we seemed
to be leaving Magical Miranda's stall. I had no problem with Magical Miranda herself, whose eyes were not
unbeautiful—for human eyes, of course. But wasn't I at
the fair to win the beauty contest? Couldn't we get that
over with and go home?

Our little party—me, Harmony, Bro, Arthur, and
Maxie—headed down the alley that divided the two rows
of stalls, me in my backpack, everyone else walking. At the
end of the alley stood two big white tents, one with farm
animals inside, the smell too obvious to even mention, and
the other with a flag at the top of the tent pole. A flag
with the face of a cat on it! Not a bad idea, not bad at all.
Around then was when Maxie said, "Catch you later, my
good buddies," and darted off to the side.

"Seventy-seven and three-quarters," Harmony said,

speaking in the quiet voice she uses for talking to herself, but Bro heard her and laughed. Meanwhile I kept my eyes on Maxie, now some distance away. He seemed to be stuffing some rocks in his pockets. That seemed odd to me.

Then, beyond Maxie, at the fence that marked the boundary of the fairgrounds, I saw another odd thing, maybe even odder. A trailer stood by the fence and two clowns were on their way inside, a red-nosed clown first, followed by a green-nosed clown. The green-nosed clown held a large wrench behind his back—I've spent a lot of time watching Elrod try to fix things, so I know a lot of tool names. Were the two clowns planning on fixing something?

Inside the tent, we had metal stands—like at the ball field in town—for the audience, still streaming in, a snack bar over in one corner, and a half circle of stools out in the middle of the straw-covered floor. Near the stools stood some people, most of them holding cats, although one was in a mesh backpack like mine, hers actually worn on the back. This particular cat—somewhat whitish, a whitishness not at all comparable to my own snowy whiteness, scarcely needs mentioning—gave me a look. I gave her a look back, let her feel the effect of my golden gaze. Her own gaze was somewhat golden as well, but a dull, unglittering golden that had no effect whatsoever, certainly not on me and therefore also not on any competent judge.

A woman stepped forward, microphone in hand. I knew this woman: She'd sold us our tickets when we came into the fair—the gum-chewing woman, although if she had gum in her mouth now she wasn't chewing it. I noticed her eyes—big and dark, kind of like Magical Miranda's.

The woman tapped the microphone, making a sound I didn't appreciate one little bit. "Welcome, everybody—two-footed or four!—to the first ever All-County Feline Beauty Contest, which I hope will be a big attraction at the fair for years to come. My name's Randa Bea Pruitt, and I'm the director of Sunshine Amusements, the company that runs the midway at this county fair and others in the Green Mountain State and all over the country. I know one thing for sure—every cat here is a winner! Have you ever seen so much feline beauty in one place? Give all of our contestants a big hand!"

Applause from the humans, plus some hollering and whistling, all of which hurt my ears. Meanwhile my new frenemy in the adjoining backpack was eyeing me in her annoying way again. I yawned. Yawning can be a nice weapon; take a little tip from me.

"Now," said Randa Bea, "I'll explain how this is going to work. First, we're delighted to have as our judge today Ms. Pamela Vance, editor of *Green Mountain Cat* magazine. After the crowd is settled, I'll introduce Pamela and . . ."

Randa Bea went on and on like that, causing me to tune out. When I tuned back in, there'd been some big changes.

First, the stands were now packed with people. Second, I was sitting on one of the stools, Harmony standing beside me. Each of the other cats was also on a stool, also with a single human beside them. My frenemy sat on the stool next to mine. Which allowed me to see her tail for the first time, a tail lacking a gold tuft at the end. The end of my own tail is golden-tufted, a striking grace note to the whole package, in my opinion.

Beside this soon-to-be loser stood her human, an old white-haired lady, perhaps on the shy side, sort of hanging back like she wasn't comfortable standing up before a crowd of her own kind. She looked my way, gave me a little smile, then leaned down and whispered in my frenemy's ear. I hear whispers very clearly, and at quite a long distance, just so you know. What the nice old lady whispered was, "Oh, dear. But there's nothing wrong with second place."

Nothing wrong with second place? I couldn't believe my ears. Of course I had to believe them: My ears never miss a thing. Human ears are a different manner. So often you hear humans saying, "Come again?" or "Can you turn that up a tich?" Sometimes they even cup a hand behind an ear to make it stick out more—not a good look on anybody— and say, "Eh?" You have to feel sorry for humans, although I try not to spend much time on that sort of thing.

". . . and then," Randa Bea was saying, "the winner and

the runner-up will have their pictures taken for the next issue of *Green Mountain Cat* magazine, over at the media space behind the curtain by the snack bar. Pictures taken, by the way, by our outstanding photographer, Cuthbert the Clown. Cuthbert—take a bow!"

Over by the snack bar, the black curtain slid open and the clown stepped out, a green-nosed clown with an enormous camera around his neck. A spotlight shone down, making his white face extra white and his green nose extra green. He leaned forward to bow, but the weight of the camera, pretty much the size of a suitcase, seemed to pull him down. He staggered, almost fell, twisted around, and fell behind the curtain, out of sight. Lots of laughter from the crowd. Was something funny? Perhaps I'd missed it.

"Ha-ha, ha-ha. And now, ladies and gentlemen, boys and girls," said Randa Bea, "please welcome the judge of today's contest, Ms. Pamela Vance!"

A spotlight shone down from above, and into its bright circle stepped . . . stepped a woman who seemed familiar. She had short blond hair, the color of the moon, and wore heavy deep-red lipstick that I almost expected would be black, and also those cat's-eye glasses. I'd seen her by night, when she'd parked outside the inn and delivered a small package to Mr. Ware. A rather busy night that had included me locking Mr. Ware out of the inn, and an owl rudely interrupting a fun game a little mousy pal of mine

71

and I were having. Am I a creature of action or of quiet contemplation? Quiet contemplation, certainly, but in action I'm . . . really something else. I'd say the same thing about myself even if I wasn't me, if you see what I mean.

Pamela Vance came into our little circle, took the mic from Randa Bea. She smiled a big smile. Her teeth were small, very white and even, and somehow sharp-looking.

"Hello, cat lovers!" she said. "I assume we've got nothing but cat lovers here."

Cries of "Yeah!" and "Yay cats!" came from the crowd. I decided that there was something to be said for this event, aside from the fact that I would soon be triumphant. Then in the front row of the stands I happened to notice Arthur sitting at Bro's feet. His tongue was hanging way way out, for no purpose I could think of, but one thing for sure: He didn't look like a cat fan. Was it unreasonable for me to expect more support from my . . . what would you call them? Followers? Yes, followers. That would do nicely.

"As editor, publisher, and owner of *Green Mountain Cat* magazine—and all our contestants will be receiving a year's free subscription, courtesy of the good folks at the magazine, meaning me . . ." She paused, gazing at the crowd as though expecting some reaction, and when there was none, her eyes darkened for a second or two, and she said, "Humor, people, humor."

Randa Bea laughed, an overloud laugh and somewhat

nervous at the same time. Pamela Vance shot her an unfriendly glance and went on. "The point is I'm a cat lover, too! And, if I may say so, an expert on cat beauty. Remember this: Beauty is truth!"

Pamela Vance began explaining how the contest would work. Or maybe not. I wasn't really listening. Instead I was thinking: Beauty is truth. Did that mean I, Queenie, was truth? Well, why not?

I fell into a pleasant mood, but it got less pleasant as the actual contest began. Not that there was any possibility of me losing. It had to do with the actions of Pamela Vance. She seemed to be going from stool to stool, gazing at the cats, giving them a pat or two—no problem so far, but what was this? Shifting an ear and peering behind it? Prodding here and prodding there? Lifting the whole being off the stool and . . . and hefting it? Shifting? Prodding? Hefting?

Me?

Pamela Vance came to the stool of my frenemy. "And what's the name of this lovely creature?" she said.

The old white-haired lady leaned into the mic. "Princess."

Well, what more was there to be said? Queenie vs. Princess. There's only one queen but you can have a whole slew of princesses. I began thinking about how to react when I was declared the winner, decided right away to do absolutely nothing.

Pamela Vance murmured, "Perfect."

Perfect? Did that murmur refer to Princess? I had a troubling thought. What if some judges were better than others? Big Fred, for example, was way handier at fixing things than Elrod, even though Elrod was the official handyman. Could it be that Pamela Vance was the Elrod of judging? Was it possible that life was unfair?

Meanwhile Pamela Vance was shifting one of Princess's rather too-pointy ears, and prodding her chest, and finally lifting her right off the stool. And all the while, what did Princess do? She purred like she was having the time of her life! For one moment I even thought Princess was about to lick Pamela Vance's face in an affectionate—even doglike!—manner. Did she actually have a dopey doglike look in her eyes? Oh, brother.

Pamela Vance stroked Princess's back, at the same time striking up a conversation with the old lady, whose name turned out to be Edna Fricker.

"Tell us, Ms. Fricker—"

"Edna, please."

"Tell us, Edna, a little bit about Princess here. For example, what's her favorite activity?"

Edna thought for a moment or two. "She likes to watch me knit."

Good grief. What could be more boring? I caught a strange look in Pamela Vance's eyes. For a moment, I thought she was going to laugh out loud, but she did not. Instead she said, "Thank you, Edna," set Princess back down on the stool, and came to me.

"And now we come to our last contestant, whose name is . . ." She held out the mic toward Harmony.

"Her name is Queenie," Harmony said.

"And yours?"

"Harmony," said Harmony. "Harmony Reddy."

"Well well," Pamela Vance said, "almost a found poem."

I'd heard that before about Harmony's name, hadn't understood it then, and didn't understand it now. From the looks on their faces, the crowd wasn't getting it, either.

Pamela Vance extended her hand, possibly to check behind one of my ears. Then, suddenly, she stopped. I wondered why. At the same time, I was aware that the fur on my back had risen straight up. And there was my answer. She'd seen the beauty of my fur and had no need for any more investigation, no prodding, no hefting. Was it possible I'd also hissed into the mic? Surely not. All those raised eyebrows in the crowd must have been about something else.

Pamela Vance turned to Harmony. "And what's Queenie's favorite activity?"

Harmony looked at me, in fact gazed at me for what seemed like a long time.

Did that seem to annoy Pamela Vance? Frown lines

appeared on her forehead. "Surely there's something Queenie likes to do," she said.

Harmony nodded. "The thing is, she has two favorite activities. One is daydreaming."

Pamela Vance's frown lines deepened. "Daydreaming?"

"She loves to lie in a patch of sun and just let her mind wander."

"How . . . interesting," said Pamela Vance. "And her other favorite activity—if we can call daydreaming an activity—is . . . ?"

"Hunting," said Harmony.

"By hunting, you mean she accompanies your father on hunting expeditions?"

Dad was in the picture? Dad hadn't been around in some time. It all went back to Mom hiring a decorator to spiff up the inn, the decorator's name being Lilah Fairbanks. Almost from the start, she and Dad had glanced at each other in ways that caught my attention, although no one else's, as things turned out. Skipping to the end of their little story, I didn't miss Dad, not one little bit.

"No," said Harmony. "Queenie hunts by herself. Indoors she goes after mice."

"And outdoors?"

"Birds."

"Does she actually . . . catch any?"

"Oh, yes. Just small ones—cardinals, robins, finches,

that sort of thing. We try to stop her, but she's pretty sneaky and . . ." Harmony came to a sudden stop, an *uh-oh* look quickly crossing her face.

All at once it was strangely silent in the tent. Birds are not so easy to catch. I'm sure the audience was aware of that, and thus suitably impressed. Once I'd actually climbed onto an amazingly high branch and taken a rather large bird, possibly a white dove, completely by surprise. You should have seen the look in its . . . but perhaps a story for later.

Pamela Vance stepped back, giving me a look that seemed quite careful. "Well," she said. "Well well." She squared her shoulders and said, "And now I'll take one last circuit around, and then decide—and what a hard choice!—on our winner and runner-up." She walked around the stools, eyeing each of my . . . comrades? Would that be it? I had a warm feeling for all of them, and if not warm, then at least not icy cold. They were getting to hang out with a champion, so this was a lucky day in their lives, even if not quite in the way they were hoping.

Now Pamela Vance was close by, gazing at Princess. At the same time, Edna was gazing at Pamela Vance, her eyes saying, *Please please please.* I came close to feeling bad for her.

Pamela Vance stepped in front of me and gave me a long look, a look that almost seemed unfriendly, but that was impossible so I ignored it. In fact, I ignored her completely. She sighed, shook her head, and then raised the mic.

"What a difficult decision! I wish there could be two winners. But since there can't, I now announce that the runner-up in the first annual All-County Feline Beauty Contest is . . . the adorable Princess! And therefore our winner . . . is Queenie."

I would have welcomed a little more excitement in the tone of her voice, but as I heard Mr. Salming say once after a hockey game, "a win is a win." As for the crowd? All the cheering and clapping anyone could ask for! Did I hear a lone cry, or possibly not quite lone, of "Princess"? Maybe, maybe not, but if so I'm sure it was drowned out by shouts of "QUEENIE! QUEENIE! QUEENIE!"

NINE

ARTHUR

WAS I LOVING THIS BEAUTY CON-
test or what? Sitting right beside us—us being
Bro on a bench seat with me at his feet—was
a wonderful family with lots of small kids, all of them out
of control. And every single one of those kids was into
snacks. They had a big-time love for Cheez-Its, Cheetos,
Fritos, Doritos—what great names!—plus burgers, Italian
sausages, Polish sausages, and even those corn dogs I'd
spotted on the way in. And the very best part? They were
messy eaters. Every single one of those out-of-control
snack-loving kids was messier than the messiest eater I'd
ever seen in my life. It was like they were having their own
contest, all about who was the champion of messy eating!
There were scraps galore! I'd had a dream like this once,
but not as good. Real life was turning out to be better than
dreams! This day was turning out nicely, so far.

As for what was going on in that circle of stools out on
the floor, I had no clue. But after a while, kind of full, at
least for the moment, I took a short break and noticed that

a sort of procession had started up, moving from the stools toward this black curtain that hung near the snack bar. This procession was led by the woman with short blond hair and deep red lipstick, who'd just been speaking into the mic, if I'd followed things right, which would have been a happy accident since, as I mentioned, I hadn't been paying the slightest attention. Then came an old lady carrying a white cat, kind of Queenie's color, and after that came Harmony carrying Queenie.

"C'mon, Arthur, let's go," Bro said.

Go? I was perfectly happy where I was, already feeling not quite so full. In fact, my appetite was starting to sharpen already. I have a great appetite, kind of like one of those champion athletes who doesn't even know the meaning of quit.

"Arthur?"

I remembered something important: I was on the leash.

Moments later, Bro and I were out on the floor, kind of bringing up the tail end of the procession, although since I have a tail and it's at the end of me, my tail was actually bringing up the tail end of the procession. Wow! I'd never had a thought like that. It was sort of . . . funny. Would another funny thought come my way soon? Or ever? I hoped so.

We came to the black curtain. The woman with the deep red lips—Pamela something or other? Had I caught that little snippet of info while hunting a totally uneaten corn dog under a seat? I thought so.

Back to Pamela, now turning to us. "Welcome to our little photo studio," she said. "And I do mean little. I apologize for the makeshift conditions. But in order to get these pictures taken properly, it'll have to be cats only."

"You mean Princess has to go in without me?" said the old lady.

"Don't worry, Edna," Pamela said. "She'll be fine. I'm a cat lover, as I said, and cats can sense it." She held out her arms, and Edna's cat—Princess, if I was on top of things—left Edna's arms and sort of glided into Pamela's arms, a glide that reminded me of Queenie, although not quite as smooth but much friendlier. Not that there's anything special about gliding. I'm sure I could glide all over the place if I wanted.

Pamela turned to Harmony, who had Queenie in her arms. "And will the winner please come forward?"

Harmony shook her head. "I don't think Queenie will—"

Pamela interrupted. "Oh, I'm sure the champ wouldn't want to miss out on having her picture on the cover of our special fall issue."

Harmony looked down at Queenie. It was hard to tell where Queenie was looking, if anywhere. It was one of those times—always annoying—when those glittering eyes were saying something I didn't understand. But a moment later, the movement so quick I'd missed it, she was in Pamela's arms. Well, just the one arm, Princess being in the other. Queenie and Princess were about the same size, but Queenie seemed much bigger. Princess's eyes, golden, yes, but not glittering, shifted back and forth. Queenie's eyes were motionless, and glittering for sure, glittering like never before.

Pamela turned to the black curtain. "Cuthbert?" she said. "All set in there?"

No answer from the other side of the curtain.

"Cuthbert?"

The curtain opened partway. And there stood the clown. I remembered him, of course, from how he'd bent down and said *Hey, little fella, have no fear.* The very next second he'd gotten all tangled up in the leash, and stumbled around like a guest we'd had last Christmas who liked Bertha's rum nogs a little too much—in short, giving me plenty to fear. I didn't feel the slightest bit pally toward this clown, and his looks were kind of alarming: those enormous floppy shoes and the big red ball on his nose being most alarming of all.

But . . . but hold on. I'd gotten mixed up. This clown, Cuthbert if I was in the picture, had a green nose, not a red one. Therefore we had two clowns going at the same time? Where was the other one? I got a bit confused. Also, was there something familiar about the scent of the man inside the clown? I knew there was a man in there, on account of the mannish smell, but the hint of cotton candy, mixed in with human male nervousness, made me think I knew him from somewhere. But where? My mind was blank, usually a pleasant feeling, but not now, for some reason. Thoughts of red and green noses got snarled in my mind, and sank slowly away.

Meanwhile Pamela was saying, "All ready for our photo shoot, Cuthbert?"

Cuthbert didn't answer. Instead he stuck up one of his thumbs, a huge thumb with a bright red nail.

"Not talking today, Cuthbert?"

Cuthbert shook his head. Pamela glanced at us. "Cuthbert has lots of silent days." She turned to Cuthbert. "What is it today, Cuthbert?" she said. "Cat got your tongue?"

Oh, what a horrible thought! I'd never heard anything more terrifying in my life! Can you imagine? Our eyes happened to meet, mine and Queenie's. Hers had a thoughtful look I never wanted to see again.

Then came another fright. Cuthbert opened his red-lipped mouth very wide and . . . and there was no tongue to be seen inside! Did a high-pitched bark of total fear sound out somewhere in the tent, possibly close by? Who could have blamed the barker? I was pretty scared myself. Then, from somewhere out of sight in his mouth, Cuthbert unrolled his tongue and stuck it way way out. Everyone laughed, meaning all the humans—Pamela, Harmony, Bro, and the old lady, called Edna, I believe. What was funny? I was still trying to get the joke when Cuthbert held out a big sort of plastic tray with sides on it, and Pamela set Queenie and Princess inside. Cuthbert stepped back through the opening of the curtain. Inside I glimpsed a camera on a stand, a big light, and a desk with some bottles on top. The curtain closed. Pamela said, "This won't take long. Why don't you all hit the snack bar, courtesy of the magazine?" She walked us over to the snack bar and handed out some sort of tickets.

We had some nice snacks at the snack bar. Everyone except for me. Pamela sat at a table some distance away, busy on her phone.

"The Frisbee contest's coming up soon, Arthur," Bro said. "And you've had more than enough already."

I had? When was this?

"Isn't this exciting?" said Edna, dipping a giant pretzel into a cup of mustard. A huge giant pretzel, far too big for any single eater to handle. I kept my eye on it. "I've never won anything in my life. I'm so glad Pamela let me know about the contest."

"She did?" said Harmony.

"After I sent Princess's picture in to Kitty Kat Korner. That's a feature in *Green Mountain Cat* magazine. Pamela emailed me about the contest. So thoughtful of her." Edna's eyes got a bit misty. "If only Edgar were here."

"Who's Edgar?" Bro said.

"My late husband," said Edna.

"What's keeping him?" said Bro.

Edna turned white.

"Bro?" said Harmony. "Late husband means he's, um, dead."

"Oh?" said Bro. Then he started turning red—kind of . . . balancing Edna turning white! What a thought! Did it mean anything at all? I didn't know. "Um, sorry, ma'am," Bro said. "I didn't—"

"That's okay," Edna said. "And in fact it's pretty funny. What's keeping him?" She started to laugh, and all of a sudden didn't seem so old and shy. They all laughed together—Edna and the twins. A small but not totally insignificant pretzel morsel flew out of Edna's mouth. I caught it before it hit the ground.

Pamela looked up from her phone. "What's so funny?"

"Uh, well," said Edna, now looking shy again.

"Not so easy to explain," Harmony said.

Pamela smiled the kind of human smile where the eyes don't join in. Mom actually has the opposite, where the eyes do all the smiling.

"So glad you're enjoying yourselves," she said. She checked her watch. "Cuthbert should be pretty much done." She headed over to the photo booth and soon came back with Queenie and Princess in her arms. "Here are the stars of the show—Cuthbert says they were perfect! We'll be sending you framed prints in a week or two. Let's see. Gold-tipped tail would be Queenie." She handed Queenie to Harmony. "And lovely pure white tail would be Princess." She handed Princess to Edna.

"The whole experience seems to have tired them out, poor little things," Pamela said, and they did look kind of limp to me. "I suggest popping them into their backpacks so they can get started on two very well-deserved naps. The celebrity life takes its toll."

The two cats got helped into their backpacks, both their tails—Queenie's gold tipped and Princess's not—getting stuffed in last. Their eyes closed immediately. The twins said goodbye to Edna and we went outside.

And there was Maxie, looking excited about something. "Where were you guys? I've been searching all over."

"At the cat beauty contest," Bro said.

"Oh?" said Maxie.

"Don't you want to know who won?" said Harmony.

"Well, not really. But I assume it's Queenie or you wouldn't have asked."

Harmony stuck out her jaw a bit, a very Bro-like move I'd never seen from her before. "Yes, Queenie won."

"Funny kind of beauty contest," Maxie said, "where the winner doesn't even know she won."

"What are you talking about?" said Harmony. "Of course she knows."

"Can't be sure," Maxie said. "Maybe if you lend her to me for a day or so I'll run some tests. But meanwhile, who wants to see something amazing?"

TEN

ARTHUR

W HAT'S SO AMAZING?" SAID BRO AS
we walked along the line of stalls.

"C'mere," said Maxie. "Check out my
pockets." He pulled his pocket openings wider. I saw some
rocks in his pockets. Was that amazing? I was missing
something, perhaps not for the first time.

"I didn't realize you were a sneak, Maxie," Harmony said.

"What a thing to say!" said Maxie. "I'm a scientist. I
investigate."

"A scientist?" said Harmony. "You just finished sixth
grade."

"A budding scientist," Maxie said.

"What's going on?" said Bro.

"Just watch," Maxie told him.

"Watch what?" said Bro.

Maxie put his finger across his lips. That's a human signal for . . . something or other. I was still hoping it would
come to me when we arrived at Magical Miranda's booth.
My tail started wagging right away, reminding me how

much I liked Magical Miranda. She said I was a good boy. Ol' Arthur doesn't forget things like that.

There didn't seem to be much of a crowd around; in fact, it was just us. Magical Miranda was sitting on a chair reading a book, and not wearing her sparkling crown, but she put it on and rose the moment she saw us.

Her huge dark eyes fastened on me. "Arthur!" she said. "One thing's for sure—you've put on weight since I last saw you!"

"But," Bro said, "that was like an hour ago. What makes you think he's put on weight?"

"Hasn't he been snacking?" said Miranda.

"Kind of, I guess, when I wasn't looking," Bro said. "But how did you know?"

Miranda smiled one of those hard-to-understand human smiles that actually doesn't look very happy. "I know county fairs," she said.

Harmony laughed. Harmony and Bro both have great laughs, and very much alike, actually kind of over the top. Miranda glanced at Harmony and her smile got a little happier.

"Enough chitchat," said Maxie. "I'm all set."

"For what?" Miranda said.

He dug some money out of his pocket and said, "For you to guess my weight. Here's my three bucks."

Miranda's deep dark eyes met Maxie's eyes, which were

not deep and dark, more like pale and sharp. The moment seemed to last a little too long, maybe got uncomfortable. At least for Bro, who looked down and shuffled his feet, a Bro thing I'd seen before, like when Mom asks if he's done his homework. After the uncomfortable moment passed, Miranda didn't seem eager to take Maxie's money. "I—I'm really done for the day."

"Done for the day?" said Maxie. "It's not even four o'clock."

"Well, on a break, then," she said.

"The show must go on!" Maxie said. "Isn't that a show-biz rule?"

When Harmony gets angry, which doesn't happen often, you can feel it building inside her. I felt it now. Her mouth opened like she was about to say something pretty force-ful . . . and then it slowly closed. It turned out I wasn't the only one who saw this little . . . how to put it? A thing not happening? That's as close as I can get. But this thing not happening was also seen by Miranda, whose gaze was on Harmony.

She took Maxie's money, but didn't stick it in her pocket, as she'd done with the money from the other customers. Instead she laid it on her chair.

"Why are you so persistent?" she said.

"Can't you guess?" said Maxie. He did one of those little laughs to himself, the kind possibly called a chuckle.

There were no other chucklers in the group, at least not then. Harmony crossed her arms over her chest.

Miranda shook her head. "I can only guess weights, Maxie."

"Then be my guest and guess away!"

"I will," Miranda said. "But first, Maxie, can I ask you to please ditch the rolled-up coins?"

"Huh?" said Maxie.

"Or the lead bars, or the boxes of screws, or the rocks, or whatever else you've got in your pockets?"

Maxie's mouth and eyes opened wide. His face turned a tomatoey color. The smells of all of them—Maxie, Miranda, Harmony, and Bro—started changing, all in different ways. So hard to keep track of! It's not so easy being a dog—don't forget that. As for what was going on, I leave that to you.

"I—" Maxie said. "I—I don't. I mean not on . . . on purpose. Sort of." He began to back away. "It's for science. I'm . . . I'm a budding, um. But there's no such thing as magic. So there must be . . . must be some trick!" At that point, backing up, he bumped into a big woman holding a giant stick of cotton candy, mostly backing into the cotton candy. Then came a commotion, and in the middle of that, Maxie spun away and took off. He turned out to be fast! People are full of surprises.

Miranda watched him go. As she did, were her eyes

starting to dampen? Yes, for sure. They dampened and dampened and overflowed, tears streaming down her face although she didn't make a sound. She took off her crown, and almost seemed like she was going to throw it away. Instead she laid it on the chair and turned her back to us, her thin shoulders shaking.

Bro and Harmony glanced at each other. They both looked shocked. Poor Miranda, a friend of ol' Arthur. That was one thing for sure. I went over and pressed my head against the side of her leg.

Miranda made a sound, kind of a sniffle. Then she wiped her eyes on the back of her sleeve, turned, crouched down, and kissed the top of my head. "Oh, Arthur," she said.

"Um," said Bro. "What's, uh . . ."

"What's wrong, Miranda?" said Harmony.

Miranda looked up at them, blinking away the last of her tears. "Nothing's wrong," she said.

"But—but—" said Bro.

"Is it because of Maxie?" said Harmony.

"Oh, no," Miranda said. "I've . . . I've seen it all. But thanks for giving me the heads-up."

"We gave you the heads-up?" said Bro.

"Just enough of a hint," Miranda said.

"Like what kind of a hint?" Bro said.

"On your faces," Miranda told him. "In your eyes. You didn't like what your friend was doing but you couldn't

92

rat him out." She wiped her eyes again. "And I don't even know your names."

"Harmony," said Harmony.

"Bro," said Bro. "We're twins, but not the identical type."

"That must be nice," said Miranda.

Harmony and Bro both looked surprised.

Miranda laughed. "Or not." She glanced up at Bro. "Is that your real name? Bro?"

"Yeah," said Bro.

"Well," said Harmony, "not strictly speaking. Our mom named me and our dad gave Bro a name Bro hates, but I think he'll change his mind one day."

"Never," said Bro.

"What is it?" Miranda said.

"Can you guess?" Bro said.

"Now you're sounding like Maxie," said Harmony.

Bro frowned. "You really can only guess weight?"

Miranda nodded.

"How did you learn?" Harmony said.

"Well, it's supposed to be magic," said Miranda. "And I was sort of a natural, but Cuthbert taught me a lot."

"Cuthbert the Clown?" Harmony said.

Miranda nodded, and checked her watch. "He should have been here by now," she said. "Cuthbert works this stall after me. Not in his clown costume, of course. Everybody does a little of everything in the carnival business."

"How old are you?" Harmony said.

"Twelve," said Miranda.

"We're eleven," Bro said.

"Been there, done that," Miranda said.

Harmony laughed that real big laugh of hers. Usually when one of the twins laughs, the other does, too, but not this time.

"You're in the carnival business?" Bro said.

"Yes."

"Full time?"

"Pretty much. We're on the road nine months of the year."

"What about school?" Harmony said.

"I do it online."

"Do you get to keep all the money?" said Bro. "All those three dollars?"

"That goes in the pot," Miranda said.

"What pot?"

"We—my mom and—well, just my mom, sort of, owns the company. Sunshine Amusements. We contract out midway attractions at fairs all over the place."

"Wow," said Harmony.

Miranda smiled a shy smile. "I've been in all the lower forty-eight states except one."

"Can I guess?" said Bro.

There was a pause and then both girls started laughing. Miranda tilted her head to one side like she was looking at Bro in a new way.

"Yeah," she said. "Guess."

"North Dakota," Bro said.

"Hey!" said Miranda.

"I got it?" Bro said.

"No," she told him. "But close. North Dakota was second last. Nevada's last. And we were never going to go there ever, except now . . ." Her eyes got a faraway look.

"How come—" Harmony began, but then a voice came out of the sky:

"And now, in the old ball field behind the big tent, the event you've all been waiting for! It's time for the first annual All-County Frisbee Fetch! So pooches—get on over there! It's going to be a barking good time!"

"Barking good time?" said Harmony. "What does that even mean?"

Miranda shook her head. "We're still trying to find a good replacement for the PA announcements."

"What happened to the old announcer?" said Harmony.

Miranda looked down. "That's a real big question." She took a deep breath. "All the PA announcements used to be handled by . . . by my dad."

"Oh," said Harmony. "And, um . . ."

For a moment, she was starting to sound like Bro. Meanwhile Bro was sounding like Harmony. "Hey, come on! We don't want to be late."

"Hurry, hurry, hurry, all you four-footed fetchers! Here's

your chance to win a brand-new state-of-the-art mountain bike for your favorite human! So get your tail on over to the old ball field!"

Miranda looked up and met Harmony's gaze. "You better get going," she said.

"But—" Harmony began.

"Harmy!" said Bro, his voice pretty loud. In Harmony's backpack, worn on the front as usual, Queenie's eyes slowly opened and then slowly closed. She looked real sleepy. Also, she smelled a bit funny, but exactly in what way I didn't know.

A youngish-looking man with long hair and tattooed arms hurled a yellow Frisbee into the air, so fast and so far it was soon just a yellow dot.

"Okay, Burner—GO!" he yelled.

Then this dog—but I'm getting ahead of myself here. First I should have mentioned that we were over at the old ball field, with spectators, including Harmony and Queenie, in the stands, and in the batting cage a whole bunch of dogs, each with a human holding a Frisbee. One of these dogs turned out to be Burner, and as soon as Burner heard "GO!" he took off.

"Good grief!" said Bro, standing beside me, like . . . like Burner had caught his eye in some way.

I watched Burner chase after the yellow dot. Was there

something special about him? He appeared to be about my size, perhaps a little on the underfed side, and his legs seemed rather long, maybe a bit too long in my opinion. As for his coat, Burner sported what might be called the sleek kind, almost certainly not as soft and comfy as mine, which Mom says is like an old tweed coat. In short, while I like just about everyone I've ever met, there really wasn't anything special about Burner.

For example, was it special how he raced across the old ball field, paws hardly ever touching down? Or how about the way he suddenly caught up to the Frisbee, sprang up high—really, not that high, certainly no higher than the roof of the cab on Elrod's old truck—and snatched the Frisbee in one clean motion, whirling around in midair and zooming back to the batting cage, where he skidded to a stop and held it out for the long-haired man to take? Was there anything special about that? I don't think you would have been impressed.

After that came other dogs—including Speedy, Jet, Bolt, Charger, Rocket, and Vroom—and other Frisbees, red, yellow, green, striped, polka-dotted, black, and white. They were all okay dogs, I suppose, but in truth even less special than Burner. What was so hard about chasing Frisbees? But more important, what was the point? It was pretty hot out here at the old ball field, and also pretty dusty. Also I happened to be feeling a bit full. What do you do on a hot and dusty day when you're feeling a bit full? You lie down, stretch out, and take it easy for a spell, don't you? So I did exactly what you would do. I lay down, stretched out, and—

"Arthur? What are you doing?"

My eyes seemed to be almost closed, just narrowed down to two slits. I peered up through those slits and there was Bro.

"Arthur! Up!"

Up? *Up* was one of those words with lots of meanings. You can be mixed up, fed up, up to here, rounded up, up in the air, hung up, rung up, stood up, up and down, high up, up high, locked—

"ARTHUR!"

—although in this particular case it was possible that Bro wanted me to get up. As I mentioned already, although I'm very much the cooperative type, I wasn't actually in the mood for getting up. A good part of life is our search for comfort, and once you finally find it, shouldn't there be a very good reason for—

The voice from the sky interrupted my thoughts. "Any contestants who still haven't competed? If not, we now declare—"

Bro raised his hand and shouted. "Wait! Wait! There's still Arthur!"

I liked the sound of that. There's still Arthur. How

nice of Bro! Still Arthur! You can count on ol' Arthur. Ol' Arthur's goin' nowhere, baby. I stretched out to the max on the soft grass, unmovable, unbudgeable, still, and always—Arthur.

Bro crouched down beside me. Hey! He didn't look too happy. I wondered why.

"C'mon, Arthur," he said softly. "I'd really like that mountain bike. Harmony's going to have one. We'll want to ride together. Can't you at least try?"

Try what? Mountain biking? How could that be in the cards? Poor Bro. He wasn't doing his best thinking.

"Just once, Arthur," he said. "I'll throw and you chase. Then you'll never have to do it again." He took the green Frisbee out of Big Fred's plastic bag and waved it in my face.

Whoa! Do that again.

Bro did it again, waving the Frisbee in my face. This time I tried to snatch it and almost did, but Bro was too quick. He pulled it away and stepped back. I jumped up, tried to snatch it again.

"Well well," came the voice from the sky. "Looks like ol' Arthur here's a competitor."

Huh? Competitor was what again? I didn't know. In fact, I didn't know diddly, whatever that means. All I knew was one thing. I wanted that green Frisbee and I wanted it now! Not only that, but I wanted to lick it and possibly eat it. That Frisbee was the most amazing Frisbee in the world. I leaped up for it. And almost got it, even though Bro now had it raised above his head.

"Arthur!" he whispered. "What's going on with you?"

Not a thing! I wanted that Frisbee and I wanted it now. What could be more obvious? I leaped again, right up to head level with Bro, but at the last second he twisted away and flung the Frisbee the farthest he'd ever flung anything, and Bro has flung a lot of objects, way too many to list here—and especially now in all this excitement. Desperate excitement! Yes, that was the answer to Bro's whispered question. What was going on with me out here at the old county fair ball field was desperate excitement. I was desperately excited to possess the green Frisbee, to have it all to myself forever and ever.

Excited excited excited desperately excited: That was what was pulsing in my mind as I chased after the green Frisbee. I hardly even noticed that I wasn't alone. Burner seemed to have joined the chase, and not only Burner, but also Speedy, Jet, Bolt, Charger, Rocket, and Vroom, plus other dogs whose names I'd forgotten or missed in the first place. But guess what. All of them—Burner, Speedy, Jet, Bolt, Charger, Rocket, Vroom, and all the rest—were eating the dust of ol' Arthur!

Because all at once, and for the first time in my life, I understood velocity. Not only that, I commanded velocity. I, Arthur, was a speed demon. I flew after the flying

Frisbee, closing in with every bound. Did I hear the roar of the crowd? Possibly not, but only because of the unusual position of my ears, sticking out straight behind me from the wind I was making. Yes, I was now commanding not just velocity, but the wind as well!

Closer and closer I got to the Frisbee, gliding in a long curve toward a big tree. Behind me I heard the pant-pant-pant of all those others, falling farther and farther behind. And now I could smell my wonderful Frisbee, fill my nose with its fabulous aroma. Just a few more bounds and—and—

But what was this? An enormous bird was hopping off a branch high up in the big tree? And swooping down in a straight line toward my Frisbee? Oh, no! I bounded one last bound with all my heart, then gathered all my strength and took to the air, really flying, flying just like a bird myself.

I snatched my Frisbee, but at the exact same moment the enormous bird snatched it, too, snatched the Frisbee in its nasty beak. We fought it out in midair, the bird glaring at me with its tiny, hot eyes, and me growling back in a way no bird would soon forget. Look at me that way, Mr. Bird? That'll only make me more desperately excited! Which was just what happened. With a last mighty twist of my head, I wrenched my Frisbee out of the nasty beak, the bird squawking and flapping off, and me gliding back to earth.

The winner! I, Arthur, winner and still champ! Well, maybe not the still champ part. But I didn't worry about that. I didn't worry about anything. All I did was lick my Frisbee, licking it like there was no tomorrow. And why should there be? Today was perfection.

ELEVEN
QUEENIE

I DIDN'T FEEL TOO GOOD. IN FACT, I DIDN'T feel good at all. For one thing, I was so sleepy. Feeling sleepy has always been a nice thing in my life, the way my body and mind just relax and relax and very soon I'm in another world, a private world of sweet dreams. The kind of sleepiness I had now wasn't like that. This was edgy sleepiness, not at all relaxed in body or mind. I even hurt a little bit. The top of one of my back legs felt like it had gotten poked. Had I been poked? I didn't remember that. I actually didn't remember much at all.

Oh, I knew I was Queenie, of course. And that I lived at the Blackberry Hill Inn with Mom and Harmony and Bro. There was also Bertha the cook, who always gave me fresh cream in the morning, and Elrod the handyman, who sometimes called me "Boss," and . . . and Arthur. What did Arthur do for me? Nothing. Would life at the Blackberry Hill Inn be better without him? Yes. But—but I wouldn't have minded Arthur's company at the moment. How strange! How complicated I am, and in such an interesting

103

way, and always totally a boss, as Elrod for one knew very well—a boss and in need of no one. But . . . where was everybody?

I opened my eyes. Uh-oh. And realized they were already open. If my eyes were open, why couldn't I see anything? Was it night? I can see pretty well at night. Was I in a dark room? I can see pretty well in dark rooms.

I sniffed the air. I smelled detergent and damp clothing and dust balls. Those were the smells of the laundry room down in the basement of the inn. I don't mean the old part of the basement where I do some of my best hunting. I mean the new part, with the laundry room and the wine cellar that Dad was building from the plans drawn up by Lilah Fairbanks, but that never got built because of . . . well, because of Mom kicking Dad out of the house. I knew it was the right thing to do, knew it just from the look on Mom's face when she told him to go. How upset she was! And that upset was all over her face. But there was another look as well—the look of a human doing the right thing.

But . . . but why was I thinking these thoughts? My mind—edgy and nervous—seemed to be wandering around on its own, like it wasn't even mine! All at once I puked. Some others of my kind are frequent pukers, but not me. I hate feeling pukey and I also hate puking. As for eating my own puke—an occasional activity of Arthur's—the idea is revolting. Actually enough to make me puke. Which I did again! Oh, what was happening to me? I moved away from the puke, but after only a step or two got dizzy—dizzy! Me! And slumped down into what felt and smelled like a disgusting pile of laundry waiting to go in the washer. I could almost hear the scene, Harmony telling Mom it was Bro's turn, Bro saying no way, followed by the same old endless and annoying back-and-forth. If only I could actually hear it now, instead of just almost.

Queenie! Stop this at once! Get a grip! Your mind is your mind and must obey. Mind! Obey!

My mind heard me and went quiet. I still didn't feel too good, but at least I knew where I was, namely down in the laundry room at home. My least favorite room in the whole place, but as long as I was home, everything was all right.

I got up, felt dizzy, slumped down, got up again, and moved toward the door. I knew where the door was in my own laundry room, no matter how strangely dark it happened to be. I reached the door, raised a paw, gave it a push. The laundry room door is made of wood. Whatever I was pushing on felt like metal against my paw, cold metal. I felt dizzy and slumped down.

Queenie was alone. Queenie loves being alone.

I didn't want to be alone.

Somewhere not far away a phone rang. The phone that rings most often at the inn is the one at the main desk. It makes a sound like br-ring, br-ring. The phone ringing now made a sound more like bzzz, bzzz.

Then came a woman's voice. Not Mom's, not Bertha's. This woman sounded much older, her voice thin and a bit scratchy.

"Hello?" she said. After a pause, she went on, "No, you didn't wake me. I've just gone to bed." Then there was a longer pause before the woman said, "I'm actually think-ing of calling the vet in the morning. She doesn't seem like herself. She's even a bit . . . aggressive."

Another silence.

"Yes, hard to believe, I know, from such a loving creature," the old woman said. "Maybe it was all the excitement. I finally put her in her special place and she hasn't budged. With a person you might say she's in a funk about the outcome, but she's not a person so . . . what? You think she knows?"

After that, a long silence. Was the old woman finished with the phone call? Who had they been talking about?

"Okay, then, talk to you tomorrow."

Then came a click, the click of a phone call ending for sure.

Somewhere far away an owl hooted. Was it my owl? The huge white one who'd made off with my mousy friend? The huge white owl was not my friend. I had a strange and horrible thought: The huge white owl was coming after me, would find its way somehow into the laundry room. I rose up and clawed at the metal door or wall or whatever it was.

A dim light shone behind me, enough for me to see that I was clawing at a washing machine. I turned my head, saw a narrow shaft of light shining through the crack under a door. I was in a laundry room, all right, but not my laundry room.

Pat pat pat. I heard the approaching sound of a bare-footed human. The pat pat pat stopped outside the door. Human listening makes no sound, but when you're near a human who's listening you can feel them doing it. I felt human listening.

And then came the voice of the old woman. "Princess? Are you all right?"

TWELVE

ARTHUR

HAIL THE CONQUERING HEROES!" said Mom.

We were out on the patio behind the inn, the evening air soft and warm, the sky all purple and fiery, everyone in a circle around us—us being me next to Bro, and Queenie in her backpack on Harmony, and everyone being Mom, Bertha, Big Fred, Elrod, some friends like Mr. and Mrs. Salming, Mrs. Hale the librarian, Mom's cousin Matty Comeau, the twins' friend Jimmy Doone, and a bunch of guests. All those happy faces! This appeared to be some sort of party, although not a birthday party since there was no cake with burning candles anywhere to be seen. Cake isn't at the top of my list when it comes to snacking, but any kind of food at all would have been good right now. I'd never been so hungry! And I knew why. I'd had way too much exercise. All that running and leaping and charging around, really enough to last me the rest of the summer and possibly all the way through winter, if I was lucky, since I much preferred the indoors in winter.

Bertha raised her glass. "Here's to Queenie and Arthur!"

Glasses got raised all around. "I can understand Queenie's victory," said Mrs. Hale. "But—pardon me—I never pictured Arthur as an athlete."

That got a big laugh. Something about me? An athlete was what again? Before I could figure that out, I got distracted by all the pats I was getting.

"Way to go, champ!"

"Numero uno!"

"Yay, Arthur!"

Ah, how nice of everyone. What had I done, exactly? I'd hopped into Mom's car all by myself when she came to pick us up at the fair, not needing my usual boost. Was that it? If that was all it took, I'd certainly do it again, although not for a bit, my legs quite suddenly feeling a little on the tired side. I wandered over to the lawn and curled up. Mom came over and looked down, a big smile on her face.

"Well well," she said, "aren't you amazing?"

I raised my tail, not very high, what with my energy level sinking fast, and let it thump down on the grass.

"I'm proud of you, Arthur. Although I'm having a lot of trouble believing it. How have you kept this talent hidden for so long?"

That was a tough one. How does anyone do anything? Don't you just sort of do it and try to understand after? Or not? Works for me.

Bertha appeared and topped up Mom's glass.

"The champ's taking a well-earned rest?" she said.

"Looks that way," said Mom. "The strangest thought has come into my mind, Bertha."

"What's that?"

"The 1919 World Series."

"The one that was fixed? The Black Sox scandal?"

"Exactly," said Mom. "But how would you fix a Frisbee contest where the competitors are dogs?"

Bertha's eyes shifted. I've come to believe that can be a sign of something going on in the human head. Lying in the grass by the patio on this warm and happy evening, I had the most amazing thought. Do my own eyes shift when something is going on in my head? Wow! Just wow! Had I gone too far? Probably.

Meanwhile, Mom was giving Bertha a very close look. I'd seen that close look before. There was only one Mom. The very best, but a real tough cookie, as I'd once heard Deputy Sheriff Carstairs say. No longer deputy sheriff, if I'd been following things recently, on account of some mess-up actually involving Jimmy Doone's cow and Queenie's missing cream, a whole big complicated case that I hadn't understood well at the time and understood less well now. As for cookies, I'd never come upon one too tough for me.

But back to Mom's very close look. Folks on the receiving

end—even folks who are pretty tough cookies themselves, like Bertha—usually get a bit flustered.

"Uh, Yvette," said Bertha, Yvette being Mom's other name, besides Mom. "What are you suggesting?"

"You tell me," said Mom.

Bertha sighed. "It wasn't my idea."

"Go on," Mom said.

Bertha turned and spotted Big Fred, somehow popping a bottle cap off a bottle with his thumbnail and handing the bottle to a guest who seemed a bit startled. Bertha made a little finger gesture and Fred came at once. They're boyfriend and girlfriend, in case that hasn't come up yet.

"Fred?" said Bertha. "Anything you want to tell Yvette?"

"Sure thing." Fred beamed down at Mom. "Thanks for the great party, Yvette. So nice of you to invite me and—"

"Uh, Fred?" said Mom. "What are you talking about? You're practically family."

"Fred!" Bertha said. "That's obviously not what I meant. I'm talking about—"

And here came a bit of a surprise. Bertha jerked her thumb in my direction. High above me their faces formed a little circle, a peering sort of circle with all eyes—Mom's, Bertha's, Big Fred's on me. Were they planning some treat for ol' Arthur? No other thought came to mind.

"Yeah?" Big Fred said.

"Yeah," said Bertha.

"Aw," said Big Fred. He shuffled his feet. "The thing is, Yvette, he really wanted that mountain bike. And of course Harmie was going to win one. I mean, jeez, Queenie. Ever seen another cat like her? Not me. So . . ." He shrugged his huge shoulders.

"So—so you . . . you gave the other dogs something in their food?" Mom said.

Big Fred tilted his head to one side. "Something in their food?"

"To slow them down," Mom said.

Big Fred put his hand to his chest. "Yvette—I would never—"

"Do something like that," Bertha interrupted. For a moment she seemed to be glaring at Mom.

And Mom's face turned a bit pink? And she looked away? I'd never seen that before, not in all the time I'd spent with Mom.

"I'm sorry, Fred," she said. "I was way out of line."

"No worries," Big Fred said. "I can see how crazy it seems. And I can't believe it actually worked. I didn't know Arthur had it in him."

"Had what in him?" said Mom.

"The physical ability," Big Fred told her. "All I was trying to boost was his motivation."

"The get up half of get up and go," Bertha said.

"Yeah." Big Fred flashed her a quick smile and she

flashed him one back. Kind of like . . . like teammates. Harmony and Bro play baseball and hockey, so I've watched a lot of games, and you see quick stuff like that sometimes between the players. So Bertha and Big Fred were kind of a team, where . . . where Mom and Dad were not. Whoa! Why would I have such a thought? I didn't even understand it myself. But I'd never seen Mom and Dad share a quick look like that.

"Gotcha," said Mom. "So what's your secret sauce for motivating this guy?" She pointed in my direction with her chin, meaning they were still talking about me. As for precisely what about me, I seemed to have lost the thread.

"You're actually pretty close," Big Fred said. "Not an actual sauce but more like a dollop of—"

Bertha leaned toward Mom and whispered in her ear, a human move for making sure no one else hears. Meaning no one else with human ears. It just so happens that I'm not human, so I could hear what Bertha was saying perfectly well.

"A dollop of bacon grease from the pan. I was frying up some of the bacon that Fred makes in that smoker of his."

"Ah," said Mom.

"I kind of improvised," said Big Fred.

"Brilliantly," said Mom. She gave me a look. "Bacon has magical power in Arthur's world."

How true! But not what you'd call an amazing thought.

Bacon has magical power, no question, but isn't that the first thing everyone learns about bacon? You're cruising along, just living your life, and then one day you run into bacon, and nothing's ever the same.

"Do you ever wonder what Arthur's thinking when he looks like that?" Bertha said.

"I know what he's thinking about now," Mom said. "Five letters. Starts with *B* and ends with *N*."

Bertha and Big Fred laughed. They were nice people so I hoped they weren't laughing at Mom for messing up. I wasn't thinking about letters at all, whatever those were. I was thinking about bacon. Specifically how at parties— and wasn't this some sort of party out here on the patio?—there were sometimes plates of shrimp wrapped in bacon, which happened to be a delicious combo. Any chance a plate or two would be appearing anytime soon? Perhaps not. There wasn't a trace of bacon aroma in the air, air that otherwise smelled quite lovely on this summer evening. I was having a good day. The truth is almost all my days are good. For no reason at all, I licked Mom's toes, bare on account of the sandals she wore.

"Oh, Arthur," she said, "what are we going to do with you?"

Just keep it up, doing what you do. For example, no need at all to move your feet right now. That seemed simple enough.

"Uh, Yvette," Big Fred said. "Speaking of what we're going to do, I hope you're not thinking of letting Bro in on our little secret."

Mom thought for a bit. "I'm guessing it was a very small dollop—otherwise Bro might have detected it."

"Tiny," said Big Fred.

"Minuscule," said Bertha.

Mom nodded. "I'll carry the secret to my grave."

Uh-oh. Whatever this was had taken a dark turn. But maybe not, because Mom, Bertha, and Big Fred started laughing, even did a bit of high-fiving.

Right then Harmony came up.

"What's so funny?" she said.

The high-fiving and laughing stopped. The adults looked a bit awkward and . . . and sort of kid-like, while Harmony was having one of those moments when she looked all grown up.

"You're laughing at Arthur?" she said. "What did he do now?"

"Not at him," Mom said. "Where's our other winner?"

"I put her on my bed," Harmony said. "She's real sleepy. Actually kind of droopy. Do you think she could've caught something, Mom? Like a cold from one of the other cats?"

"Is she sneezing?"

"No. And she's actually being very affectionate. She even licked my hand."

"I don't believe it," Mom said.

"It's true."

But I didn't believe it, either. Queenie? Affectionate? That was not the Queenie I knew. Also the Queenie I knew had a different smell from . . . from . . . I got a little lost.

Meanwhile Mom was saying, "Probably worn out from all the excitement. Let's see how she is tomorrow."

"Okay, Mom."

"Looking forward to riding that brand-new mountain bike?" said Big Fred.

"Oh, yeah," Harmony said. "They're getting delivered in the morning." She gazed down at me. "I still can't believe what he did."

There was a silence. Then Bertha said, "It is pretty incredible."

They all nodded. My takeaway? I was pretty incredible.

Later that night, I bedded down in Bro's bedroom, first beside the bed, then on it, and after nothing I'd call an actual dispute over who got which pillow, me or Bro, I settled into one wonderful dream after another. Such as a dream where Burner was eating my dust. Sometimes dreams can come true! Was I even dreaming or back at the fair and charging across—

Someone was in the room. My ears went up right away. Then I smelled who it was: Harmony. No lights were on out in the hall, but I could see her form, the moving part of the darkness. She came close to the bed.

"Bro?" she said very quietly.

No answer from Bro. His chest rose and fell in that slow, easy rhythm of a happily sleeping kid.

"Bro?" Harmony said a little more loudly.

Still nothing from Bro.

"Bro!" She jabbed at his shoulder.

"Wha—" said Bro, sitting up real quick.

"Bro! Get up!"

"Huh?"

"Get up! Now!"

"Is something wrong?"

"I can't find Queenie."

"Huh?"

"Bro. I need you."

Bro rubbed his eyes, swung his legs over the side of the bed. He was wearing the same clothes he'd worn during the day, shorts and a T-shirt. Harmony had on pajamas.

"Queenie's, um . . . ," he said.

"Missing," said Harmony. "She was sleeping beside me. I woke up a little while ago and she was gone."

"Probably on the grandfather clock," Bro said, and started to lie back down.

"Bro! You think I didn't look there? I tried all her usual spots. I even went down to the old cellar."

"Gross."

"That's not the point. She's been acting so strange since we got home. I'm worried about her."

"Do you think she went outside?"

"Maybe."

Bro stood up. "Then we better take Arthur."

"Why?"

"So we can track her."

They both gazed down at me.

"I suppose anything's possible with Arthur now," Harmony said.

Did you hear that? What great news! Certainly something to look forward to when I woke up in the morning, or afternoon, whichever the case might be. I rolled over, closed my eyes, and felt sleep on its way, just around the corner.

"Arthur?" said Bro. "Up and at 'em."

Up and at 'em? What kind of sense did that make? Wasn't it night? Night is the time for sleep. Don't get me wrong. There's plenty of good sleeping to be had in the day. But when it comes down to it—

"Arthur!" said both twins at once, a sort of whispered shout, very unusual and a bit alarming. I yawned a huge yawn, trying to send the message about night being good for sleeping and me being a bit on the sleepy side, in the hope that—

"Get up!"

■ ■ ■

A warm summer night, with soft breezes and a big round moon, not so bad if you had to be up and about, which seemed to be the case. We walked behind the inn, Bro, me, and Harmony, side by side, moonlight putting a silvery sheen on everything—the shuffleboard court, the trees, the garden shed, and the faces of the twins. Hey! Their faces looked kind of worried. I wondered why.

"Arthur," Bro said. "Do you smell Queenie?"

What? This interruption of my badly needed sleep had something to do with Queenie? That was a turn for the worse.

"Arthur!" said Harmony. "Try."

"Sniff the air," Bro said. "Do that scent thing you do."

Scent thing? Did I need to sniff the air to do that scent thing? I did not. All I had to do was breathe, and I was already breathing.

"Find Queenie, Arthur," Bro said.

"Please," said Harmony.

Poor Harmony. She sounded upset. No way I wanted that. This was about Queenie? I breathed in a nice breath, full of interesting smells, including the smell of a flower that's not in the air during the day. Was there some Queenie in that breath? Yes, but not a lot, and not particularly fresh, and there was always some Queenie scent around the inn, on account of the fact, recently discovered

119

by me, that Queenie sometimes went on outdoor excursions at night. Just to be nice, I followed a weak little trail of Queenie scent until it petered out, then wandered around a bit, picked up another one, and at that moment heard a distant splash.

I paused, head up.

"Did you pick up her scent, Arthur?" Bro said.

"Take us to Queenie!" said Harmony.

Queenie? This had nothing to do with Queenie. This was about a distant splash, coming from beyond the apple orchard, where there was nothing except the old wishing well and the falling-down stone wall between our land and the back road. Sometime in the past, Mom got the idea of fixing up the old wishing well in case guests might like to take their pictures in front of it, as well as throw in money, if I'd understood Mom right, and she and I had made several trips out there and worked hard to fix it up, but not many guests ever went and none threw money. The money part ended up being wishful thinking on Mom's part, and—Whoa! Was that why they called it a wishing well? Because you wished people would throw money in it but they never did? Wow! Was I starting to understand humans at last? What a night!

"Bro?" said Harmony. "What's he doing?"

"Well, pointing, kind of," said Bro.

"Meaning he's picked up on something?"

"With a well-trained dog, yeah, but we can't really—"

"Arthur!" Harmony bent down so we were face-to-face. How fine she looked in the moonlight, although very upset. "Please find Queenie."

That was it! Queenie! I forgot all about the wishing well, the faint splash, wishful thinking, and started following this new scent trail of Queenie's, no stronger than the last one. It led in a long circle, around the garden shed, where—

Ah. This was interesting. Queenie's faint smell merged with a just-as-faint mousy smell, not far from a wheelbarrow. I stood over the small patch of field grass where the two scents were mixed together, and saw a short shoelace type of thing, which turned out to be a . . . mouse tail? Queenie could be . . . I wouldn't want to say dangerous, but she could be shockingly quick, and her claws—as I knew from a single one-time event that would never be repeated—were shockingly sharp.

"Has he found something?" Harmony said.

"Not that I can see," said Bro. "I'll bet a dog peed here. That always gets his attention."

Well, of course it does! Good grief! But no dog had peed here, not in a long, long time. I love Bro, but take my word for it, not his. I stepped away from the mousy smell, which quickly vanished, although Queenie's smell did not. It led me toward the side of the house, where it sort of flowed into a whole bunch of other smells, including more recent ones of Queenie's, and brought us right to the door.

"So Queenie was outside and now she's back in?" Harmony said.

"I don't know," said Bro. "Let's see what he does."

Bro opened the door. I went in. What I was going to do was climb the stairs to the family quarters and get back to what I'd been doing, namely enjoying a good night's sleep, but I smelled something odd. Not Queenie exactly, but . . . odd. The scent came from down the stairs, not up. I started down. The twins followed, not saying anything, but I could feel that I had their attention.

We stepped down into the basement, not the old scary cellar but the new nice part. The first door you come to leads to the laundry room. It was open and I went inside, following the odd smell.

Bro flicked on the light. It shone on a pair of golden eyes, looking up from a pile of dirty laundry on the floor.

"Queenie!" said Harmony. "What are you doing here? Have you ever even been in this room?"

"She looks kind of weird," Bro said.

I thought so, too.

"Maybe she should see the vet," Bro went on.

"First thing in the morning." Harmony moved toward the laundry pile, but stopped at the sound of footsteps behind us. We all turned.

And there in the doorway stood Mr. Ware, his wild white hair wilder than ever, and his shirtfront a little damp.

"Oh, hi, everybody," he said. "I just got back and I'm afraid I got a bit lost in your beautiful but somewhat confusing inn." He glanced around. "Is there a problem? Maybe I can help."

This . . . this cat we had in the laundry room began to purr. I'd heard Queenie purr, but only when she was gazing at herself in the mirror. Still, it was a nice, friendly sound. I could probably get used to it.

THIRTEEN
ARTHUR

BRO'S MOUTH OPENED AND CLOSED. Harmony's mouth opened and she said, "Thank you, Mr. Ware. No, there's no problem."

Mr. Ware peered into the laundry room. "Your cat looks mighty cozy." His voice sounded older and scratchier than ever. Mr. Ware confused me. I tried to sort out everything I knew about him in my mind, but my mind didn't seem interested in helping. What my mind wanted to do was just think about the Frisbee contest and never stop. I'd fought a big nasty bird for possession of that Frisbee and I'd won! Thinking about the Frisbee contest was way better than thinking about Mr. Ware.

"Cozy?" Bro said. "I'm not so sure she's—"

Harmony broke in. "Bro, would you mind showing Mr. Ware the way up to his room?"

"Uh, sure." Bro turned to Mr. Ware. "What room are you in?"

"The Daffodil Room, I believe."

Bro nodded. "It's real easy. Go back down the hall till

you come to the stairs, and then two flights up, hang a left and—"

"Bro?" said Harmony. "Can you take him?"

"Take him?"

"Show him the way."

"But—"

"That's how Mom likes it done."

"Okay," Bro said. Which was the right answer. How Mom likes things done was how they always ended up getting done.

"I wouldn't want to make work for anyone," Mr. Ware said. "If I can be useful here with this cat situation, I—"

"Bro doesn't mind a bit," Harmony said. "Do you, Bro?"

Hey! Did Harmony just sound a bit like Mom?

"I guess not," said Bro. "This way, Mr., um—"

"Ware," said Mr. Ware, who had by now pretty much crowded into the laundry room with the rest of us.

Bro stepped into the hall. Mr. Ware followed him, and I followed Mr. Ware. If this was how Mom wanted it done, then that was that. We headed down the hall and came to the stairs. Bro switched on a light and we went up, Bro, Mr. Ware, and then me. One thing about old people: They don't climb stairs like young people. But Mr. Ware did climb stairs like young people, smooth, quick, easy—in fact, not so different from a cat. My mind left off thinking about the Frisbee contest and got ready to do some serious thinking about Mr. Ware. It was still getting ready by the time we came to the guest room floor and stopped at the door with the yellow flower.

"Here you go," Bro said.

"Many thanks." Mr. Ware took out his key. "You seem to be having a busy day."

"Kind of," said Bro.

"Anything to do with your cat?"

"Partly, I guess. Queenie won the cat beauty contest at the fair today."

"Ha-ha. No surprise there." Mr. Ware opened the door. "She's a real beauty, isn't she?"

"Yeah."

"And now she's worn out from all the attention?"

"Maybe," Bro said. "Or she's sick. We'll probably take her to the vet in the morning."

Mr. Ware paused in the open doorway. "Oh?" he said. "Do you have a good vet?"

"Yeah."

"Always nice to have a good vet. What's his name?"

"It's a her," said Bro. "Dr. Tess."

Mr. Ware nodded, and then without another word stepped into the Daffodil Room and closed the door. Click went the lock.

I lay down, right outside the Daffodil door. The carpet was nice and soft, would do very nicely as a bed for the night.

Bro looked down. "What are you doing?"

I stretched out, sending the message that I was fine. Go on back to bed, Bro. I'll just settle in here, not because of the softness of the carpet—comfy, yes, but not nearly as comfy as our bed, mine and Bro's—but because . . . because . . . The truth was I wasn't particularly sure about the reason. It just felt right.

"Arthur? Arthur. Arthur!"

There are many ways of saying my name, some harder to ignore than others. I rose, and Bro and I made our way back through the house to the family quarters. Harmony was already there, headed into her room. Golden eyes gazed at me over her shoulder. Purring started up. She was purring, just from the sight of me? I could get used to that.

"Harm?" Bro whispered, what with Mom's room being down at the end of the hall. "Do you hear that? What's going on with her?"

"She's just so happy that she won."

"Yeah?"

"What other reason could there be? But she does feel a little warm to me." Harmony patted the head of our purring . . . guest? Was that what she was? "You're seeing Dr. Tess in the morning." Harmony carried the guest into her room and shut the door.

Not long after that, we were bedded down, me and Bro. We each have our own pillow, but I always end up liking his better, hard to explain why. Soon Bro was fast asleep, and I was on my way, closer and closer and . . . did I hear some footsteps, in the house but somewhat distant? I wasn't sure. I listened for a bit, heard nothing—well, maybe a car started up, somewhere or other—and then sank down and down into a lovely dream, all about snacks and running very very fast.

"You're right," Mom said. "She does feel a little warm. On the other hand, all this purring—it's so unlike her."

I opened my eyes. Sunshine was streaming into our room. Morning already? That was quick. I rolled over. Bro was already up, standing out in the hall with Mom and Harmony.

"But purring's good," Bro said.

"I don't know," said Harmony. "Maybe she's trying to tell us something."

"Like what?"

"Let's see what Dr. Tess has to say," Mom said. She took out her phone. "Hi, Yvette Reddy here. Our cat Queenie doesn't seem well. Could we bring her in to see Dr. Tess?" She listened. "Really? I see. Thanks. Bye."

Mom turned to the twins. "They'll have to call back," she said. "Dr. Tess isn't in yet and they're not sure when she's arriving. Car problems. Well, actually it looks like someone let the air out of her tires overnight."

"A prank?" said Harmony.

"If so, a very mean one."

At that moment, Bertha called up the stairs. "Harmony and Bro? Someone here to see you."

We went downstairs, and there in the front hall was a complicated scene. We had a person I recognized, namely Randa Bea Pruitt, the woman who ran the fair. Then we had another person I didn't recognize at first. This person was a girl wearing jeans and a baggy sweatshirt. She seemed a bit familiar, with those long braids and big dark eyes. Big dark eyes, like Randa Bea's but even bigger and darker. Got it! Magical Miranda! A sparkling gown and a sparkling crown would probably make anyone look different. I cut myself some slack for not recognizing her right off the top, cutting yourself some slack being almost always the best move.

But there was more than Randa Bea and Magical Miranda, because also in the front hall stood two shiny bicycles, one red and one blue, with fat tires and big bows tied to the handlebars. Humans have a certain way of standing when they're trying not to hop up and down, which was how the twins were standing now.

"Oh, boy," Bro said.

"Oh, boy, oh, boy, oh, boy," said Harmony.

And then came a lot of jibber-jabber where Harmony

was introducing Mom to Miranda, and Miranda was introducing Mom to Randa Bea, who turned out to be her mom. Had I already known that? If so, I really knew it now.

Not long after that, the twins and Miranda had taken the bikes outside and Mom was in the dining room with Randa Bea. Bikes or dining room? That was my choice. I took dining room.

No guests. You look for guests right away when you're in the B and B business. Guests like to sleep in. I'd make a very good guest in someone else's inn, but why would I go there? Ours was the best.

Mom and Randa Bea sat at Mom's favorite table, the little round one in the back corner, with windows on two sides. Mom was pouring coffee when I went over and sat by the table. Had Bertha come to take their order yet? Mom usually had yogurt and fruit. Maybe Bertha had gotten Randa Bea interested in her maple-smoked sausages. That was my hope.

Randa Bea peered down at me. "Don't take this the wrong way, but I'm trying to think of some famous athlete—even one—who didn't look athletic."

Mom laughed. I wasn't sure why. Were they talking about me? I was an athlete, of course—nothing could now be clearer—but was I famous?

"Sure can wag his tail," said Randa Bea. "I'm so glad I added the Frisbee contest. We were only going to have the cat beauty contest at first."

"Oh?" said Mom.

130

"Pamela suggested it."

"Who's Pamela?"

"Pamela Vance—publisher of *Green Mountain Cat* magazine. A great idea. But then I thought—why not dogs?"

"An Arthur-type thought," Mom said.

They laughed. I noticed I was still wagging my tail. Well well. My tail is almost like a . . . a sort of . . . little Arthur on its own. What a strange thought, and somewhat frightening. I sat down on it at once, got things under control.

Randa Bea sipped her coffee. "Mmm. Very nice."

"Thanks," said Mom. "That's our medium roast. We switch things up from week to week. A surprising number of our guests turn out to be coffee connoisseurs."

Randa Bea nodded. "The ups and downs of dealing with the public."

"It's mostly ups," Mom said.

Randa Bea looked around. "Your inn is lovely. And the town, too, from what I've seen. Are you from around here?"

"No," said Mom. "But my ex-husband was. We bought the place thirteen years ago. It was pretty much a ruin back then."

"Ex?" said Randa Bea.

"Yes."

"So now, if you don't mind my asking, you're the sole owner?"

"Me and the bank," said Mom.

Randa Bea smiled. "The bank part goes without saying. It sounds like you and I are sort of in the same boat, except you seem farther down the river."

"Oh?" said Mom.

Randa Bea put down her cup, leaned slightly forward. "How did you get your ex to give up his half? Did you buy him out?"

"Couldn't have afforded to," Mom said. "But he didn't really put up much of a fight."

"Why not?"

Mom thought about that. "I'd like to believe because he'd lost his moral standing and knew it."

"Moral standing?"

"He was—and is—having an affair. With the interior decorator I hired to do the final spiffing up of the inn, as it happens."

Interior decorator? The only interior decorator I knew was Lilah Fairbanks, not a fan of dogs, as it turned out. She wasn't around anymore on account of something to do with Dad, and he wasn't around, either. I got the feeling I was following this conversation between Mom and Randa Bea very well. Ol' Arthur was on a roll, no question! My tail got loose and thumped the floor. I rounded it up pronto and let it know who was boss.

"So because of that he felt ashamed and willingly let go of his share of the inn?" Randa Bea said.

Mom met her gaze. In my world, when we meet another one of our kind, we size them up. Was something like that happening now?

"Or there's theory number two," Mom said. "He's swept up in a new adventure and is just too excited to care."

"No flies on you," said Randa Bea.

Kind of a weird comment. Yes, we had flies in the summertime, but Elrod had installed brand-new screens in the spring, and the odd fly that managed to sneak inside got whacked with Bertha's swatter. There was not a single fly in the whole dining room—I'm very good at smelling flies, by the way, fly scent being strong and rather unpleasant, in case you didn't know.

Meanwhile Mom laughed a very little laugh. "I'm much sharper after the fact."

"Say hello to your twin sister," said Randa Bea.

I glanced around. No one had entered the dining room. Did Mom have a twin sister? Why was I just finding that out now? Harmony and Bro were twins, of course, but not the identical kind, as Bro tells everyone they meet. Had Randa Bea gotten herself a little mixed up? It had to be that. I gave her a pass. Getting mixed up happens in life. Sometimes in bunches!

"Although," Randa Bea went on, "you seem to be handling things much better than me. In my case—" Randa Bea's phone buzzed. She took it from her pocket, glanced at the screen. "Terribly sorry," she told Mom. "I have to take this." Then, into the phone, she said, "Any news?" She listened. "Try that cousin of his in Connecticut." She clicked off and shook her head. "And now the clown has disappeared."

"The clown?"

"Cuthbert. That's his clown name but we all call him that in real life, too. He was supposed to deliver the bikes with Miranda and he didn't show up, which is why I'm here. Clowns tend to be unpredictable in my experience, but we've had no problems with Cuthbert. Naturally Marlon never liked him, god knows why."

"Marlon's your ex-husband?" Mom said.

"Not quite ex, since the divorce is pending. It's just been a mess." Randa Bea gazed into her cup. "I inherited Sunshine Amusements from my dad. After my mom died, I took over for her, meaning I basically ran the show, my dad having . . . some problems. Then, when I married Marlon everyone said I should have a prenup agreement keeping one hundred percent ownership in my hands, but that seemed like such a coldhearted way to start a marriage." She looked up. "On the other hand, the business side of me knew it made sense. So in the end the contract I never paid much attention to—but I signed it, god help me!—turns out to be full of holes. And Marlon is taking advantage of every single one. Through his lawyer, of course. Marlon himself is always traveling and unavailable." Randa Bea drummed her fingers on the table. "Traveling with Ms. X, I assume."

"Ms. X?" said Mom.

"There's a Ms. X and has been for some time," Randa Bea said. "I don't know her name. Marlon denies the whole thing, but he's slipped up a few times, including once when a friend of mine saw the two of them at a restaurant in Reno. I confronted him. He called my friend a liar. She's a close, longtime friend. I kicked him out."

"Close longtime friends are good," Mom said.

"You betcha," said Randa Bea. They clinked coffee cups. "Can I ask how your kids are handling the divorce?"

"On the surface, pretty well," Mom said. "They've got each other, of course, and they're both really into sports, meaning lots of physical exercise. As for what's going on inside, I'd say that Harmony's pretty much taking it in stride. I suspect Bro is very angry at his dad, but he doesn't say so. I tried to get him to open up about it a few times. No go. But in my experience when people seem basically happy, they usually are, and he does."

Randa Bea took a deep breath, let it out slowly. "Miranda's an only child. Not interested in sports. Very different from your son. But the same in not wanting to talk about it."

"I hear she's amazing at the weight-guessing attraction," said Mom.

Randa Bea nodded. "The way it's usually set up—with three-pound margins on either side, meaning a six-pound window altogether—means a trained person has a high success rate. But Miranda hits the exact number so often that I let her say within one pound in her spiel."

"How does she do it?"

"Meaning is it on the up and up?"

"I wouldn't want to put it quite that way," Mom said.

Randa Bea smiled. "Carny history is full of attractions that weren't on the up and up, but Sunshine Amusements isn't like that. Miranda's uncanny, simple as that. Like an iceberg a lot of the time, mostly below the surface."

"Sounds like a very interesting person," Mom said.

"Thanks," said Randa Bea. "What I worry about—"

Whatever Randa Bea was worried about I missed completely. Why? Because one of our guests came into the dining room, a newspaper under his arm. It was Mr. Ware. He glanced around, a quick, sharp-eyed movement, those sharp eyes partly hidden under the shaggy white eyebrows, and spotted us at the table in the corner. Mr. Ware stopped dead. Then, fast and silent, he backed out of the dining room and disappeared. But not before I noticed he had a small scratch on one cheek.

I had half a mind to follow Mr. Ware, check out what

he was up to. The other half of my mind was still hoping for maple-smoked sausages. While those two halves were fighting it out, Harmony came hurrying in.

"Mom? Dr. Tess is here. She stopped in to see Queenie on the way to work."

FOURTEEN

QUEENIE

I DIDN'T FEEL TOO GOOD. FOR A WHILE
I'd been feeling better, but now I wasn't.

Once we'd had a very old guest at the inn. He didn't
say much, mostly liked to sit in the shade by the shuffleboard court and watch people play, which actually didn't
happen often, shuffleboard proving to be not very popular.
From the top shelf of the armoire in the Big Room I have
a good view of the shuffleboard court. I happened to see the
old guest get off his chair one morning and shuffle off, if
that's how to put it. He ended up getting lost and Deputy
Sheriff Carstairs didn't find him until nightfall. "Some old
people get confused," Mom told Harmony and Bro. "It's
very sad."

And now it seemed like a confused old person—in this
case a woman, possibly named Edna, whom I suppose I'd
met but paid no attention to—had entered my life. That
didn't make me sad. I felt annoyed. For one thing, she
seemed to think I loved the closeness of dirty laundry. For
another, she kept calling me Princess. I knew Princess,

of course, an also-ran in the beauty department. Anyone who could get us mixed up had to be very confused indeed.

"Princess?"

Here she was again.

"I've brought you some of that Fancy Bite kibble! Your favorite." She set a small metal kibble bowl by me on the floor.

First, I did not care for that bowl at all. It just so happens that my kibble bowl matches my cream saucer, white china with a gold border, of a type I believe is called Sèvres, the saucer and bowl the last remaining pieces from a set that had been in Mom's family for a long time. And now, this cheap, dented, crummy piece of tin? Please.

Second, the kibble itself smelled disgusting. I turned up my nose.

The old lady stood nearby wringing her hands.

"You're behaving so strangely," she said.

Oh? Me? I really had had enough of this old lady. I checked my surroundings, found I was no longer in the laundry room, although I had no memory of leaving it. Now I seemed to be in a small musty den with a lot of woven stuff around—on the couch and the chair, hanging on the walls, much of it frayed. I knew who was responsible for the fraying, was suddenly in the mood to do some fraying of my own. As for the room itself, it was just like the tin bowl. I hated it.

Time to make tracks, Queenie. I rose. Or at least started to. But my legs didn't seem to have it in them. How odd! I settled back down on the floor, a wooden floor with the odor of Princess sunk deep in the boards.

"Oh, dear," said the old woman. "How about I pick you up and we have a nice little cuddle?"

Excuse me? Did I hiss, or perhaps show my teeth? Well, wouldn't you? Whether I had or not, the old lady burst into tears and left this dreary room, closing the door behind her.

I looked out the window. Nighttime. One small lamp shone in the far corner, leaving most of the room in shadows. Fine with me. I would have preferred darkness to this room. First choice, of course, was my own place, the Blackberry Hill Inn. The window—the only one in the room—was open, but there was a screen. A closed, unbroken window was impossible. Closed screens were usually impossible as well, although not always. Sometimes they had a little hole in them, a little hole that could be made bigger. I rose.

Or at least started to.

What was wrong with me? Was I thirsty? Yes. I noticed—how had I missed this?—a water bowl placed close to the kibble bowl. Here's something basic about me and my kind. We do not like the water bowl and the kibble bowl to be close together. How could this old lady,

Princess's companion after all, not know this? Did it have to do with the old lady's confusion? Or some failure on Princess's part?

Probably both. Often, in this life, there's plenty of blame to spread around.

Meanwhile I was thirsty. Problem one was the bowls being too close together. Problem two was that the water bowl didn't match the kibble bowl. Yes, it was metal and crummy and dented, but the metal of the kibble bowl was a dull silvery color, the metal of the water bowl more coppery. I like my bowls to match. Is that too much to ask?

Problem three: I couldn't get up.

There are several kinds of sleep, at least for me, dozing being one of them. Dozing is nice if you want to be in two worlds at once, the world of dreams and the world of every day. At the same time, you're getting some rest, although not as much as when you're deep in the world of dreams. But I had the idea that being completely absent from the everyday world might not be completely . . . I don't want to say safe, because I'm not easily scared—oh, how I hate that expression *fraidy-cat*! Whoever thought it up doesn't know us at all!

But I'll say *safe* anyway. It was safer to stay at least a little in the everyday world. So I dozed.

And as I dozed, the house changed around me, settling down for the night. The inn's a big house and the night changes are many and go on for a long time. This seemed more like a small house. There were one or two creaks from somewhere, the sound of a toilet flushing, water flowing in the pipes, pat pat of bare feet on the floor, slow-moving feet of someone not very heavy or strong. Then came a soft human groan, muffled sounds of bedding being adjusted, the click of a light switch.

And a sigh.

Time passed. In the dreamworld I hunted mice, down in the old cellar. In the everyday world I was thirsty. More time passed. I found myself sipping from the crummy water bowl.

But in which world? Dream or everyday?

I took another sip. Dream water would taste perfect. Water from a second-rate bowl would still taste second-rate, no matter how thirsty you were. This water tasted second-rate. I was in the everyday world, an everyday world lit by a single weak lamp in the corner, its light dirty yellow, and everything it touched a bit dirty yellow, too. I glanced down at my gold-tipped tail, to see if it was now dirty yellow—and got a terrible shock. A shock I hadn't come close to dealing with before I realized I was not alone.

Not alone, because there was movement outside the

open window. It was very dark out there, some shadows still, some on the move. Then came a metallic snip-snip-snipping sound, and a big square section of the screen folded in on itself and fell silently into the room.

Some creatures are quick in neither body nor mind. I'll leave you to come up with an obvious example. Other creatures are quick in one but not the other. And then there are the quick in both body and mind types, such as myself. Right now, my mind knew at once: Now is your chance to escape! Leap through the opening in the screen and race through the night, all the way home!

But my body was not itself. I couldn't get up. I wasn't feeling too good.

Meanwhile, just outside, one of the shadows emerged from all the others and became a man. This man— a man I knew—climbed through the hole in the screen. An unusual man: He could be young or old. Tonight, he was young. He came toward me making hardly any sound, his movements almost as silent as those of me and my kind. A large sort of gym bag hung over one of his shoulders.

"Well well," he said softly. "You seem to have landed on your feet." He bent toward me. "Come on. I'm taking you somewhere nice."

I did not want to go anywhere with this man. He leaned down and down, a smile spreading across his face. I did not like that face or that smile. I did not like his breath, sickening breath that reminded me of cotton candy. From somewhere deep inside, I found my last little bit of strength, just enough to take a swipe at that smiling face.

"Ow!" he cried—rather loudly, I thought—then reeled back, the smile gone now, and felt his face. Ah, some blood, not a lot, but enough to make a gratifying sight. He went still, listening with his full attention. The house was silent.

"Ow," he said again, but now in a whisper. He dabbed his face once or twice. "Now why would you want to do a thing like that? I value our friendship, even if you don't." He held out his hands. "Now come."

Come with him? That was not going to happen. If he came the slightest bit closer, I'd—

But he did not come closer. Instead his eyes narrowed slightly, eyes that had turned dirty yellow in this strangely lit room, and he spoke, or rather made a sound. "Meow."

A perfect meow. It touched me, way down deep, in a way I can't explain. All I could do was sit still and allow him to pick me up.

"There you go, my beautiful thing," he whispered.

His dirty-yellow eyes gazed into mine. I gazed back. I hardly noticed the appearance of a needle-like thing, hardly felt its sting.

■ ■ ■

Darkness, darkness, and I didn't feel too good. All was black, but I knew it was daytime. Day smells different from night.

A car door opened, not far away. A woman got out. A woman's footsteps are different from a man's. She took a few steps. Then someone farther away said, "Dr. Tess?"

That someone was Harmony! Oh, how happy I was to hear her voice. Harmony, my Harmony.

"Had to buy four new tires," Dr. Tess said. I knew her, of course, perhaps not my favorite human, but far far up the scale from my . . . my kidnapper. Which is what he was. "Just crazy that someone would do a thing like that," Dr. Tess went on. "But I thought I'd drop by on the way in, see how Queenie's doing."

"Oh, thank you," said Harmony.

Dr. Tess's footsteps moved toward Harmony. Then both sets of footsteps moved . . . moved away? In the exact wrong direction from me?

But I'm here! Queenie's here! Harmony! My Harmony!

A door closed. I knew the sound of that door closing very well, had heard it so many times. It was the front door of the Blackberry Hill Inn. I was home.

And not home. From around the side of the house came other footsteps, a man's. They crunched across the gravel parking lot, crunch crunch. A car door opened. The space

I was in sagged down a bit. The car door closed. The engine fired. I sensed movement. And put it all together. I was in the trunk of a car and we were driving away from my home.

From in front came the faint smell of cotton candy.

FIFTEEN

ARTHUR

HELLO THERE, ARTHUR," SAID DR. TESS. We were in the kitchen at the inn—me, Mom, Harmony, and Bro. Plus our golden-eyed guest, now lying on a blanket near the table. I knew Dr. Tess, of course, but only from visits to her office. Now here she was visiting us. Had I stepped on a thorn again and didn't even know it? I checked my paws, not by licking them or anything like that, but sort of just with my mind. Wow! Just with my mind! I was getting better every day.

But what was the point? Where was I going with this? Um.

Um.

Oh, right. My paws felt just fine. So what was Dr. Tess doing at my place?

"Hmm," said Dr. Tess, looking at me more closely. I looked at her more closely, but couldn't keep it up. "Didn't we put you on a diet last visit? Have you been sticking to it?"

"That's on me," Mom said. "I promise to be more vigilant."

"But Mom," said Bro. "So what if he's a little on the husky side? He won the Frisbee contest, didn't he?"

"What?" said Dr. Tess.

Bro told Dr. Tess the whole story of the Frisbee contest. He missed a few details, such as the bacon grease part, but just the same it was thrilling to hear.

"Wow!" said Dr. Tess, giving me a quick head scratch, an absolutely expert head scratch. "Amazing," she said.

"Yes indeed," said Mom.

Dr. Tess shot her a quick glance. Why? I had no idea. Mom gazed into the distance.

"How about this, Bro?" Dr. Tess said. "Let's try to stick to the diet and maybe he'll perform even better."

Bro thought about it. "Okay," he said.

Dr. Tess smiled. "And now let's see the patient."

She walked over to the blanket, which was when I knew for sure I wasn't the patient. Were things going my way these days? This was how to live.

Dr. Tess eyed the patient. "Hmm," she said. "Hmm. And what's Queenie been up to?"

"She had a big day yesterday as well," Mom said.

"Oh?" said Dr. Tess. "Let me guess. She won the cat beauty contest."

"Hey!" said Bro. "How did you guess that?"

Dr. Tess smiled at him. "Like all guesswork, I suppose. I stood on the facts I had and made a mental leap."

148

Mom and Harmony laughed, so something funny must have happened. Bro and I seemed to have missed it. We're real good buddies, me and Bro. The best.

"But since the fair," Mom said, "she's been out of sorts."

"How?" said Dr. Tess.

"Listless," said Mom.

"And purring a lot," Harmony said. "She's not a purrer, so what does it mean?"

"Is she eating?"

"She tasted the kibble and didn't seem to like it."

"Drinking?"

"Maybe a little. The level in her water bowl went down but I didn't actually see her drinking."

"So it could have been Arthur?"

What was this? All eyes were suddenly on me? What had I done?

"I've never seen him drink from Queenie's bowl," said Bro.

Me? Drinking from Queenie's bowl? Never! Well, once. I didn't even want to think about that incident. Over in a flash, but afterward! My nose! She'd come out of nowhere, possibly flying down from the top of the fridge, and caught me a good one. The sting lasted for days and days. In short, it had been a long time since I'd gone anywhere near Queenie's bowl. I was innocent! I looked up at everyone with the most innocent eyes I could muster.

"Looks guilty to me," Harmony said.

"I'm afraid so," said Dr. Tess. "Maybe Queenie picked up some bug at the fair. Let's start by taking her temperature. Anything from one hundred point four to one-oh-two point five is good, but Queenie is always one-oh-one on the nose."

She opened her bag, took out some sort of gizmo. "This goes—very gently, of course—in her ear until it beeps. Queenie tolerates it very well, as I recall. Mind holding her for me, Harmony? Firmly but not roughly is the way to go. Careful she doesn't scratch you."

Harmony bent down and lifted our guest into her arms, where she curled up and purred some more.

"Well well," said Dr. Tess. "She's making it easy today." Dr. Tess stroked the patient under her neck, at the same time slowly sticking one end of the gizmo in the patient's ear. "Now we wait for the beep."

While we waited, Dr. Tess gave the patient a careful look, from the tips of her ears to the tip of her tail.

"That gold tip is just incredible," she said. "The icing on the cake."

"That's exactly what I thought the first time I saw her," said Mom.

"The color is so . . . so vibrant," Dr. Tess said. "I've never—"

Beep beep beep.

Dr. Tess slid the gizmo out of the patient's ear and checked its little screen. "One-oh-two point four. A normal reading, although on the high side for Queenie." She turned to the patient. "Anything bothering you under that glorious coat?" Dr. Tess stroked the patient's back, down to her tail, her fingers sort of exploring all the way—back, legs, tail, the golden tip.

"It feels a little . . ." Dr. Tess went silent. With her fingernails she sort of picked a bit at the tail, the way Bro sometimes picks at me when he's checking for ticks. "So odd," she said, and then she raised her hand. Between her finger and her thumb, she held a tiny gold flake.

"What's that?" said Harmony.

Dr. Tess looked at Harmony, a look maybe not of the friendliest kind. "Gold paint," she said.

"Paint?" said Harmony, Bro, and Mom, all at the same time.

"Spray paint, most likely," Dr. Tess said. "Some people think it's amusing or cool to spray paint a cat. Or . . . or maybe to enhance some feature that's already there. Perhaps the temptation of a beauty contest was a bit more than—"

Harmony interrupted. For a moment she looked just like Mom—in fact, even more so, if that makes any sense. "What are you saying?"

"I think I know what Dr. Tess is saying." Mom looked

Dr. Tess in the eye. "No one here would ever do such a thing."

Dr. Tess met Mom's gaze, at least for a bit. "I'm not suggesting that."

"Huh?" said Bro. "I think you—"

Mom held up her hand.

Dr. Tess held up both of hers. "If I did, I'm sorry."

Mom nodded, a nod that means we're moving on.

"But whoever did it," Dr. Tess said, "is no friend to cats. Is there any vegetable oil? And a bowl of warm, soapy water?"

Soon Dr. Tess went to work on the patient's tail with vegetable oil and warm, soapy water. After not very long at all the famous golden tip was gone, leaving the tail snowy white from beginning to end. What was going on? I had no idea.

"She's an imposter!" Harmony said.

"What does that mean?" said Bro.

"This isn't Queenie," Harmony said.

They looked at each other. Sometimes I get the feeling that Harmony and Bro can speak to each other silently— which happens all the time among me and my kind, by the way.

"It's Princess?" said Bro.

Harmony nodded.

Ah.

SIXTEEN

ARTHUR

THINGS BEGAN HAPPENING FAST, AND that can be a problem when it comes to remembering them later. So I may be leaving out some of those fast-happening things, even important ones. But what can you do?

I'm pretty sure of the first thing, namely Dr. Tess saying, "You're absolutely right, Bro! Princess is one of my patients." Then came a lot of talk about how she'd sensed something was off from the start, and how Princess's temperature always ran on the high side of normal, and how Princess's temperament was "more outgoing" than Queenie's. Which was one way of putting it.

"But," Dr. Tess said, "I don't get it. What's going on? How did you kids come home with the wrong cat?"

"A wrong cat disguised as the right one," said Mom.

They all went silent, gazing down at Princess, curled up on the blanket, eyes closed to tiny slits. That tiny slit expression was a Queenie look, and one of her most annoying, and the two of them were pretty identical to the

153

eye—except for the gold-tipped tail issue, which I didn't understand at all—but I don't go by the eye, at least not right off the bat. What do I go by? The nose, of course! And their scents, Queenie's and Princess's, were different. Very hard to explain how, but if you had my nose, you'd have known right from the start—just like me—that the cat we brought home was not Queenie.

"Why would anyone do a thing like that?" Dr. Tess said.

"I don't know," said Mom.

"But," said Harmony, "if Princess is your patient, then you know where she lives."

"She belongs to Edna Fricker, over in Stockville." Dr. Tess got busy with her phone. "Forty-nine Indian Ridge Road—that's just after the bridge. I'll call her right now."

"Um," Bro said.

"He's right," said Harmony.

About what? Had Bro even said anything? I was confused, and Dr. Tess looked confused as well. On Mom's face was a more complicated look, maybe a bit confused, but there was also love in it.

"It's better," Harmony said, "if we just go over there and knock on the door."

"Are you saying you suspect Edna?" Dr. Tess said. "But of what? Switching the cats? But why? She adores Princess."

There was a silence. Everyone—including Princess, which was very strange—turned to Mom.

"Let's go knock on her door," Mom said.

We went outside and Dr. Tess placed Princess in the very back space of Mom's car. At first I got the idea that Dr. Tess was going with us, but then a call came in about a sick horse and she headed for her office instead. Harmony and Bro had a discussion about who was riding shotgun, solved as usual with rock-paper-scissors, a game that was incomprehensible to me, but not to Harmony, who always won, and we all jumped in. Including me, on the back seat with Bro. Mom glanced at me in the rearview mirror.

"What's Arthur doing?" she said.

"Looks like he wants to come," said Bro.

Mom's eyes stayed on me for another moment or two. "At least we know we've got the right Arthur." She turned the key.

The right Arthur? Was there a wrong Arthur? What would he be like? I thought about that for a bit and got nowhere.

Mom likes to drive with the windows open. Even in winter, she doesn't quite close her window completely. One more reason to love Mom. Is it because she loves smelling all the smells whizzing by, just like me? Maybe not: I've actually never seen her stick her nose out the window, the way I was doing now.

And oh, what smells! Here are just some: squirrel, rabbit,

pizza, suntan lotion, fox, those little yellow flowers, cigarette smoke, human sweat, pee—pee, pee, and more pee, many many kinds—corn, apples, burnt rubber, more flowers, the red ones, more pizza, rat, mouse, stinky sneakers, and pee. Pee pee pee, and then we were parking in front of a small house with many hanging plants on the porch.

Mom gazed at the house. "Let's leave Princess in the car for the time being," she said.

"As a bargaining chip?" said Harmony.

"Too soon to put it that way," Mom said.

We got out of the car, walked up the steps of the porch, with Bro in the lead, kind of striding. An interesting sight, but I had no time to think about it. Bro knocked on the door.

"We're just knocking," Mom said. "Not breaking it down."

I heard footsteps in the house, from somewhere in back.

"Maybe no one's home," Bro said.

What can I tell you about human hearing that won't hurt your feelings? I'll keep my opinion to myself.

Bro knocked again.

From inside the house came the voice of an old lady, a voice I recognized. It was Edna. Voices stay with me for some reason.

"Just a minute," she said.

The door opened. There was Edna, maybe smaller

than I remembered. Her glance swept over us, settled on Harmony. "Harmony?" she said.

"Where is Queenie?" Harmony said.

Edna put her hand to her chest. "Oh, no. Don't tell me she's missing, too?"

"What are you talking about?" Mom said.

Edna looked up at Mom and blinked. "Princess ran away," she said. "I've been searching and searching. She's nowhere to be found."

"Ran away when?" said Mom.

"Sometime during the night. She—she broke out through a screen. That's so unlike her. She just hasn't been the same since—"

Harmony interrupted. "Do you mean last night?"

"Yes," said Edna. "I can't tell you exactly when. I was asleep. I was so exhausted, what with worrying about—"

"Last night?" Bro said, his voice rising. "That's not possible."

Uh-oh. Was Edna some sort of problem for us? I moved in a little closer in case Bro wanted me to . . . to bite Edna, for example. I'm not much of a biter, but if biting was what Bro wanted, I'd do my best.

"Oh, dear," said Edna, stepping back and starting to tremble.

Mom raised her hand. "I think we've gotten ourselves a little sideways."

What did she mean by that? To bite or not to bite? That was the question.

"Edna, is it?" Mom said. Edna nodded. "I'm Yvette Reddy, mom of these two."

"I've already put that together, thank you," said Edna.

"Well, nice to meet you, even under these odd circumstances," Mom went on. "Would you mind winding things back to when this all began? Say, after the photo session at the fair?"

Edna shrugged. "Pamela Vance, the nice lady from the cat magazine, went to get the cats from the photographer and brought them over to us. I took Princess home. She was very sleepy and also a bit unsettled. The truth is she hardly ever leaves the house. So her restlessness was no surprise, the excitement of the day and all. I've got a very tall armoire that she's always completely ignored, and suddenly now all she wanted to do was climb right up to the tip-top. I put a stop to that, of course—"

"Why?" said Bro.

"How?" said Harmony.

Edna leaned back a bit, like she'd been caught in a strong wind.

"Never mind all that," Mom said. "Continue with your story."

"After the . . . the incident at the armoire, I noticed that she was gnawing at her tail. That was a first, and very upsetting, so—"

"Was there anything unusual about her tail?" Mom said.

"Why, no."

"The color was normal?"

"The color? Princess's color—snowy white. But it was upsetting to see her so unnerved, which was why I took her down to her comfort place—that's the laundry room—and left her there for a while, hoping she'd take a nap and wake up more like herself."

"And did she?" Mom said.

"Not really," said Edna. "So later I brought her up to the den and offered her a nice big bowl of Fancy Bite kibble. She adores Fancy Bite kibble but now she turned up her nose at it. I sat with her, just knitting quietly, passing the time as we usually do, and her eyes finally closed. When I got up in the morning, she . . . she was gone."

"Did you search the house?" Mom said.

"Certainly," said Edna. "Although it was easy to see what had happened—the window in the den was open on account of it being summer, but the screen was closed. Would you believe she'd torn out a whole big section of the screen and escaped? I never dreamed she was capable of something like that."

"Did you search outside the house?" Mom said.

"For over an hour," said Edna. "I also called animal control but they haven't picked up any strays last week. By now she's had lots of time to—"

Bro cupped his hands to his mouth. "Queenie!" he shouted. "Queenie!"

Edna backed up another step. "I—I don't understand. What's going on?"

"Come this way," Mom said. She headed for the car. All of us followed. Me last, just in case Edna decided to make a run for it. Did she think she could outrun an athlete such as myself? Good luck with that.

And maybe Edna got the picture, because she made no attempt to flee. Mom took out her key fob, pressed a button. The rear hatch of the car popped open. Mom gestured for Edna to take a look inside.

Edna took a look inside. "Princess? Princess!"

Princess rose up, came forward, stepped into Edna's arms, where she curled up, purring.

"Oh, Princess, my Princess!" Edna's eyes got all watery. "You found her?"

"Sort of," said Mom.

"But why didn't you tell me right away?"

"She doesn't get it, Mom," Harmony said.

"What don't I get?" said Edna. "And please don't talk about me in the third person."

Mom gave her a little nod that meant okay. "We've had Princess the whole time since the fair," she said. "And you had Queenie."

"But . . . but that's impossible. I'd know my Princess

anywhere—and that's without their tails being so different. Why, anyone could tell them apart."

"Maybe you'd know Princess anywhere—" Mom began.

"And maybe she wouldn't," said Harmony.

"For sure," Bro said.

"Kids!" said Mom. "But, Edna," she went on, "someone spray-painted the tips of their tails to mislead us."

Edna peered down at Princess's tail. "That's her normal tail!"

"It was gold-tipped when we brought her home," Mom said. "A kind of gold that got washed away by vegetable oil and warm, soapy water."

Edna's mouth opened, closed, opened again. "I had Queenie the whole time?"

Mom nodded. "And Queenie's quite capable of escaping through various windows and screens. Please show us where she got out."

We headed around to the back of Edna's house, everyone walking except Princess, very relaxed in Edna's arms. Why did cats get carried all the time when everyone else had to get by on their own power? Every now and then you hear a human say, "Life isn't fair." Now, at last, I got it! This roll I was on looked like it was never going to end.

"Here's the window," Edna said. "You can see how the screen is torn."

"Wow!" said Bro.

"How did she take out a chunk that big?" Harmony said.

Mom gazed at the opening and said nothing. Then we started wandering around Edna's small backyard, fenced in on two sides, with woods at the back.

"Do you think she headed home?" Harmony said.

"Probably," said Mom. "But it's a long way. Maybe we can pick up her trail." She turned to me. "Arthur? Do you smell Queenie?"

"Find Queenie," Bro said.

"Come on, Arthur," said Harmony. "Please."

Find Queenie? Was that what they wanted me to do? For a moment I thought: What would life be like at the Blackberry Hill Inn with no Queenie? My own life, for example? But it was a short moment. If Mom, Harmony, and Bro all wanted me to find Queenie, then that's how it was going to be. And in fact her scent—not just much different from Princess's but also much stronger—was here in Edna's backyard. I roamed around in a little circle, picked up Queenie's scent trail, and followed it onto a narrow dirt path that led into the woods. I also picked up some human scent—specifically male human scent—that I knew, but was that the assignment? No. Therefore I forgot about it immediately. I really am a good good boy.

And right away everyone—except Edna and Princess, waiting behind—was saying the same thing.

"He's onto something! Good boy, Arthur!"

And lots more of that. So nice. Meanwhile Queenie's scent track stuck right to the dirt trail, making my job easy peasy. We followed it through the woods to a gravel road.

I stopped, sniffed around, made a circle and then a bigger one. Queenie's scent got mixed into a strong car exhaust smell and vanished. The exhaust smell led toward a curve in the gravel road. I followed it for a while, but sniffed not a single whiff of Queenie. I did pick up a very faint hint of cotton candy, kind of wrapped in a thick package of car exhaust, if you get what I mean.

A cloud came and covered the sun. My tail drooped down onto the road. We stood around.

"Maybe she got home already," Harmony said.

"Let's go see," Mom said.

Bro gave me a pat on the way back to the car. My tail rose. Had I somehow done a fine job without even knowing it? That was my takeaway.

We went home.

"Queenie! Queenie! Queenie!"

But there was no Queenie. I parked myself in the front hall, kept my eyes on the top of the grandfather clock, waiting for her to appear. I'm a pretty hard worker, maybe a fact about me that's not widely known.

Meanwhile, at the front desk, Mom was on the phone.

"Randa Bea?" she said. "Something's come up you

should know about." And she started in on a long, complicated story involving Queenie, Princess, the cat beauty contest, Edna, gold paint, and lots of other stuff that sounded familiar. Now, hearing it so clearly from Mom, I knew one thing for sure: She was brilliant. It was finally all clear to me, too! And then not.

On the other end, I could hear Randa Bea. "Oh my god! I just don't understand this at all. I'd better call Pamela Vance."

Mom hung up. She gazed into the distance for a while, her eyes dark and troubled. Despite how worn out I was, what with the Frisbee contest and then all this searching around for Queenie, I rose, went around the front desk, and leaned against her leg.

She looked down at me. "Something's going on, Arthur. But what?"

Good question. I was still turning it over in my mind when the phone buzzed.

"Yvette?" said Randa Bea on the other end. "I spoke to Pamela. She's just as shocked as I am. All she knows is that she gave the two cats to Cuthbert, who took them behind the photo curtain and handed them out when he was done."

"Did you tell her Cuthbert's gone missing?"

"I did. She was shocked by that, too."

SEVENTEEN
QUEENIE

WHEN WAS I GOING TO START FEEL-
ing right? Would I ever feel right again? What
a horrid thought! I'd felt right all my life, so
right that I didn't even know I was feeling right. I just
assumed that was what being Queenie felt like. Was I still
even Queenie if I went on feeling like this, so bad? And if
I wasn't Queenie, who was I?

I curled up. For a while I'd been on the move. This was
in the trunk of a car. It hadn't taken me long to figure that
out. Then the trunk had popped open and I'd sprung—

But no. Before I could actually get started—me! Who
had never even had to think of getting started!—a black
cloud was thrown over me, and strong hands wrapped me
up tight in the black cloud and carried me away. I struggled inside the cloud—not a cloud, I soon realized, but
some sort of blanket, as I could tell from the woolly smell
and the scratchy feel—and tried to claw and bite.

That brought an angry grunt from whoever had me, and
then I felt another of those sharp pokes. I became part of

165

the black cloud and stayed in the cloud for a long time. Finally the cloud turned wispy and vanished. My eyes opened, and I found myself where I am now.

How to describe this place? Is it a closet? Maybe. It has shelves, although with nothing on them, and the kind of louvered door you sometimes see on closets, where light comes slanting in through the slats. Mom's a big believer in louvered doors, especially for the closets where the guest room bedding gets stored. I'm also a big believer in them. Back at the inn, if I happen to find one of those doors open, I almost always slip in for a little lie down. Once someone passing by closed the door, trapping me inside. Later that day a search started up. "Queenie! Queenie! Where are you?"

All I had to do was meow, but I took my sweet time. It was nice to have everyone searching for me. Goes without saying, really.

Was anyone searching for me now? I listened my very hardest. Silence, as far as my ears could hear. But were my ears at their best? Probably not. My head was all fuzzy inside. I climbed up to the top shelf in the closet and lay down. Perhaps I was too tired to reach the top shelf but I did manage to reach one of the shelves. My eyes closed.

A phone buzzed.

"Yeah?" said a man, so near that the fur on the back of my neck stood straight up.

I heard, very faintly, the voice of the person calling on the other end. A woman? I thought so, but wasn't sure. I knew the man, this very bad man who sometimes spoke as an old man, sometimes as a younger one, and sometimes— and those were the scariest—like one of my kind. Right now, he was speaking in the young man voice. Not a real young man, more like a man Big Fred's age, for example. Oh, how wonderful if Big Fred came strolling in!

But he did not. Instead my enemy—because surely that was what he was—said, "When's his flight? What? Not till then? Why?"

He listened. "The price? He's dickering about the price? It was set!"

On the other end, the woman's voice rose, but I still couldn't make out the words.

The man's voice rose, too. "Hasn't he seen the photo? The tip of the tail doesn't show? That's crazy! I made sure—"

The woman's voice rose some more. She was very angry. I thought I recognized her voice but couldn't quite place it. Maybe if she'd been less angry, I would have. Most humans, in my experience, don't sound like themselves when they're angry.

The man spoke more quietly, like he was giving in. "Just let me know."

No more talk after that. I heard him moving around, heard a bottle cap getting snapped off a bottle, even heard the fizzing of whatever was in the bottle. Then things grew silent again.

A ray of sunlight shone through the slats, dust motes swirling in it, dust motes that turned gold in the sunlight. Had there been mention of a tail in the phone conversation? My tail?

I didn't know. But I felt the need for a little comforting, and what was more comforting than the sight of my golden-tipped tail? Just imagine how you'd feel if you had one.

I shifted my position slightly, bringing my tail into view. And oh, the shock! The horrific, dreadful, sickening shock! My golden tuft, the gorgeous glittering tip of my proud and lovely tail, was gone! I don't mean the tuft itself was gone. Maybe I'm not describing this too well. Please forgive me. It's the best I can do at the moment. What I'm trying to get across is that while my tuft was still there, it was no longer golden, but white, just like the rest of me.

And not even just like the rest of me. There was something off about this whiteness, something strange. My poor little heart began pounding in my chest, like . . . like it wanted to get out. To get out and find the real Queenie. Oh, what was happening to me? I had to do something, but what?

With a quick flick of my tail I got the tuft in my mouth. What was my plan? To bite it off? I really hope not. And in the end I merely nibbled a bit.

168

How odd. My tail tuft didn't taste like me at all. Not only that, but it didn't taste like cat or any other living thing. It tasted like . . . paint. A flake lodged on my tongue. I stuck my tongue out, uncurled it, and the flake dropped onto the wooden shelf beside me.

A tiny white fleck of white paint. I peered at my tuft. Almost all of it was this new strange white, except for one tiny patch of gold. My first thought: That was all that was left of Queenie, one tiny patch of gold you could hardly see. A very sad thought, but somehow I felt a little better.

EIGHTEEN
ARTHUR

B RO?" MOM CALLED. "BRO? WHERE
are you?"

"In the garage," Bro called back. And I was
with him, although he didn't mention that part, maybe
because of how hard we were working. We'd taken the
mountain bike completely apart, even though it was brand-
new. There were pieces all over the place, and Bro had a
grease smear on his nose. I'd had one, too, but Bro wiped
it off on a rag.

"Let's not shout from place to place," Mom shouted.

"Okay."

"That means come here."

"In a bit."

No answer from Mom. Bro got back to work, wrench-
ing at things, a screwdriver held between his teeth. I love
when Bro holds things in his mouth. I myself had the rag in
my mouth, the same one he'd wiped my nose with. That's
how hard we were working. We're buddies, me and Bro,
no question.

Mom stepped into the garage, an empty wicker basket in her hand. "In a bit?" she said.

"Uh," Bro said. "Argle urgle."

"Take the screwdriver out of your mouth."

Bro took the screwdriver out of his mouth. "I was on my way."

Mom didn't appear to be listening. She was looking at the mountain bike parts on the floor.

"What are you doing?"

"Customizing the bike."

Mom nodded like that made sense. "But right now," she said, "I need you to go pick a dozen ripe tomatoes. Bertha's going to make us some gazpacho."

"What's that?"

"You know perfectly well."

"That cold soup?"

"Exactly."

"I like hot soup."

"I'll bear that in mind. Ándale!"

"What about Harmony?"

"She's out tacking up those missing cat posters."

Bro thought for a moment. "Is Queenie missing, Mom?"

"Of course. What kind of question is that?"

Bro shrugged. "It's not like a normal missing cat thing."

Mom gave Bro a long look. "No, it's not." She handed him the wicker basket.

■ ■ ■

Bro reached out for a tomato. "Too hard." He tried another. "Too soft." And another, this one big and fat. He plucked it off the vine and put it in the basket. "What's the point of cold soup?" he said.

I didn't know. My only soup experience involved hot broth. Was broth even soup? I didn't know that, either. This particular broth was turkey broth, a specialty of Bertha's for the day after Thanksgiving, left in a huge silver tureen in the small parlor for guests to serve themselves—all of which I learned after the fact, or never. The huge silver tureen sat on a table—not a very high table, more like one of those quite-low coffee tables. Maybe I'd better leave these little memories right there.

Meanwhile we were down at the tomato patch, between the old barn and the dirt-road shortcut into town, picking tomatoes and putting them in the wicker basket, Bro doing the actual physical work and me supervising. Supervising is the human term for when you sit around watching other dudes work.

It was a hot day and Bro was sweating a bit. I myself had found some shade at the far end of the tomato patch and had no complaints about the heat or anything else. Then it hit me. Had I been in the tomato patch fairly recently? If so, why? My mind kept niggling away, trying to come up with some memory or other. I was considering a short nap to make the niggling go away when I noticed that Bro was watching me. Was something wrong?

"Thanks for winning me that bike, Arthur," he said.

No, nothing wrong. I loved Bro and promised myself to win him a bike every chance I got.

He got back to work. I wriggled around in the dirt, got super comfortable, and my eyes were beginning to close when I heard, right through the ground, a soft thump-thump-thumping. It's hard to sleep with a thump-thump-thumping going on in your ears, so I rose and looked in the direction of the sound. A runner was coming up the road, not a particularly fast runner like . . . like me, for example, but steady. As she came closer, I recognized this runner, maybe from her long swinging braids. It was Magical Miranda.

I barked.

Bro turned and saw her. She saw him and waved, a graceful little motion. Bro made a sort of wave that was more like chopping air. Miranda left the road and came jogging over toward us. Her face was flushed. She wore shorts, T-shirt, sneaks, a bracelet with a silver heart locket, and seemed smaller than before, and not so magical, more like a normal kid.

"Hi," she said.

"Hi," said Bro.

"Is Harmony around?"

Bro shook his head. "She's putting up posters."

"About Queenie?"

"Yeah."

"My mom told me the whole story," Miranda said. "I just don't understand."

"Me either," Bro said.

"Cuthbert's not like this. Yes, he's a clown, and he's worked in carnivals for a long time, so he's kind of unpredictable, like my mom says. But he's not mean."

"So you're saying?" said Bro.

"The cats got switched. That was mean, so a mean person must have done it. And the only person who could have done it was Cuthbert. See the problem?"

"Maybe he's mean after all," Bro said.

"I've known him all my life," Miranda said. "He's gentle. He cries when he's happy."

"So he can't be mean?"

Miranda gazed at Bro with her big dark eyes. She started looking more magical. "Don't you get a feeling when people are mean?"

Bro shrugged.

"You must have met some mean people in your life," Miranda said. "What about that friend of yours, the one with the rocks in his pockets?"

"Maxie? He's not mean."

"No?"

174

"He's real smart."

"So? Last night some of the crew guys caught him inside the fair after closing. He had one of those metal detector wands and he was wanding it all over the ground at my booth."

"I don't get it."

"He was searching for some sort of secret underground scale," Miranda said. "To prove I was cheating."

"What did they do to him?"

"Just sent him home."

"He must have been scared out of his mind," Bro said.

"Actually not. They told me he gave them some lip. All about them being enemies of science." She gave Bro a sidelong look. "Still think he's not mean?"

"It's more like he's . . ." Bro fell silent. He stood still for a moment or two and then bent down and plucked another tomato from the vine.

Miranda gazed at it. "That looks good."

"You want it?" said Bro.

"I don't have anything to carry it in."

"You could eat it here."

"Yeah?" said Miranda. "Just out of my hand?"

"Why not?" Bro said.

"I've never eaten a tomato right off the vine."

Their eyes met. Bro had a thought. He started to say something, stopped, then finally got it out. "I won't tell," he said.

Miranda laughed. He handed her the tomato. I expected she'd take just a small bite to test it out, but the bite she took was real big, almost half the tomato. Tomato juice ran down her chin.

"See?" said Bro.

"I do." Miranda polished off the other half. "Mmm, mmm," she said. Their eyes met. "Bro's short for brother?"

"I guess."

"So if I looked at your birth certificate it would say 'Brother'?"

"I don't know," Bro said. "I've never seen my birth certificate." He got this look on his face that sometimes comes when he's having fun. But nothing fun was happening that I could see. "Does yours say 'Magical Miranda'?"

Miranda laughed again, but this laugh didn't sound particularly happy. "I'm starting to hate that magical part."

"Yeah?"

She took a deep breath. "It was my dad's idea, the whole magical thing. Fun at first, just like my dad."

"Your mom and him own the carnival?" Bro said.

"Not anymore," said Miranda. "Or maybe not. They're fighting about it. Well, the lawyers are fighting. My dad's gone away somewhere with some woman. My mom doesn't even know who." She rubbed her bracelet, the one with the silver heart locket. "They're getting divorced."

Bro nodded. I myself didn't get it at all. We don't have divorce among my kind.

176

"My mom knows who," he said.

"Your mom knows who my dad went away with?" said Miranda.

"Huh?" Bro said. "No. She knows who my dad went away with."

Miranda nodded. "So we're in the same boat, you and me."

"Except I don't have any magical powers."

Miranda smiled. "You come out of nowhere, don't you, Bro?"

"What does that mean?"

"Nothing," Miranda told him. "I never thought I had magical powers, either, but now I sort of do."

"Yeah?"

"It's the only explanation."

"For what?"

"For how crazy good I am at guessing people's weights. Cuthbert taught me how to do it originally, but now I'm way better than him. Here's something you won't believe."

"What?"

"When I look at a person, I can sort of see the face of a scale inside them, the same kind of scale we've got in the booth. I just read off the number where the needle's pointing."

"Can you see the scale in me?" Bro said.

"I don't want to do that," said Miranda.

"Why not?"

"I just don't."

There was a silence. A bee buzzed around the vines. I kept an ear on it, if that makes any sense to you. Bees can be a problem. Once I came across one just sort of sitting on an apple core near the woodpile, an apple core that was actually mine, which was why I pawed at the bee, just letting him know what was what. There turn out to be many surprises in life, some bad.

"Cuthbert hates my dad," Miranda said. "And now he's done this thing with the cats and disappeared. On top of everything, he's probably Mom's most important employee. And he loves her! I just don't understand."

"He loves your mom?"

"Not like that, Bro." She thought for a bit, then took off her bracelet. "Cuthbert and my dad worked together in a circus years ago. My dad was the lion tamer."

"Yeah?"

"Here he is—my dad, Marlon Pruitt," she said. She opened the silver heart. "Me, my mom, my dad, all smiles. Not even that long ago." She snapped the heart closed.

"I . . . uh . . ."

"You don't have to say anything," Miranda said.

Bro gave his head a little shake. Was his brain getting tired? I know that one very well. "None of this has anything to do with Queenie," he said. "Well, it does, I guess, but not about where she is now. She's out there somewhere, trying to get home." He looked all around.

"What's that?" Miranda said.

"The old barn," said Bro.

"Have you searched it?"

"Why would Queenie stop there if she was so close to the house?"

"Couldn't tell you," Miranda said. "Who knows how cats think?"

Bro nodded. "Okay," he said.

We left the tomato patch, took the hard-packed narrow path through the meadow to the old barn. All the way there, and the whole time we searched the barn, finding no sign of Queenie, I couldn't get Miranda's question out of my mind, maybe the most important question I'd ever heard. *Who knows how cats think?* Wow! If only I was the one who knew how cats think! Arthur, cat expert of the world!

We left the barn.

"What's over there?" said Miranda, pointing.

"The apple orchard."

"And that thing beside it?"

"The old wishing well," Bro said. "It's from before we got here. The water's no good."

"Wishing well?"

"And no one wishes there, either."

"I want to see," Miranda said.

We walked over to the old wishing well. The opening was made of stone, but the little roof was gone, only a few rotted support beams still standing. Miranda peered in.

"I don't see any water," she said.

"It's way down there," Bro said.

That was true. I could smell it. And Bro was also right about the smell: not good, not good at all.

Miranda closed her eyes.

"Are you making a wish?" Bro said.

"If I tell it won't come true," Miranda said. "You must know that."

"But you have to throw something away." Bro took out a coin, the second smallest of the silver ones. "Here."

Miranda opened her eyes and took the coin. "Don't look," she said.

Bro turned away. Miranda stuck the coin in her pocket, then held the bracelet with the silver heart over the well and dropped it in. Silence, silence, silence. And then a very faint little splash.

Not long after that, it was time for Miranda to go back to work at the fair. Bro and I headed to the tomato patch. We were almost there when for no particular reason I glanced back. And what was this? A person stepping out of the apple orchard and moving toward the old wishing well? I barked. The person, quite far away, but bigger than a stick figure, quickly turned my way and then ran back into the orchard, out of sight.

I barked again.

180

"Knock it off, Arthur."

I barked louder.

"What? What?"

Bro stopped, looked all around. "I don't see anything. Come on."

I considered running back to the apple orchard, but it was a long way, the day was hot, and there'd been plenty of physical activity already. Besides, the person I'd seen had a very distinctive running style, where his elbows went way out from his body. There was only one person I knew who ran in such an elbowy way: Maxie Millipat. And of course Maxie was a friend of the family.

NINETEEN

QUEENIE

KNOCK KNOCK, NOT FAR AWAY. A door opened. My enemy spoke in his young man voice. "What are you doing here?"

"Is that how you're saying hello?" said a woman.

Did I recognize her voice? Had she been on the other end of a phone call while I was in this . . . this bedding closet, if that's what it was? A bedding closet I was still inside, by the way, with sunlight, not so strong now, still streaming through the louvers. Yes, possibly I knew this voice from . . . from what we might call happier times, but in those happier times did I pay close attention to every human voice that happened to come along? No, I did not, which was perhaps one of the reasons those times were happy! Ah. I seemed a little sharper now, more like myself, as though a strange and very un-Queenie-like fog was lifting in my mind. And in this state of sharpness I had a very un-Queenie-like thought: *I'm in trouble.*

"Sorry," my enemy was saying. "I'm a bit tense at the moment. But . . . but hi, babe. It's good to see you."

The door closed. Then came the sound of what I believe is called a smooch. Not a long one.

After that the woman said, "No need to be so tense, Marlon. Everything's going as planned."

Marlon. Aha. My enemy had a name. I heard him take a deep breath and slowly let it out. "You're right," he said. "You're so good for me. You calm me down."

"The only thing I don't understand is how you got Cuthbert to cooperate," she said.

"I told you—I paid him off."

"I know. It's just that he's so loyal to her."

"Loyal or not, Cuthbert's gone away on a well-earned vacation," said Marlon. "Everyone has a price—a tired old saying but it happens to be true."

"Oh?" said the woman. "What's yours?"

Marlon's voice got a bit prickly. In fact, there was always prickliness in it, sometimes well hidden, sometimes not. "What's that supposed to mean?" he said.

"Just what it says—what's your price?"

"Know something? You're a hard woman."

"That's what you love about me," she said.

He laughed, a short, barking sort of laugh. The barking part didn't resemble Arthur's bark. It was much harsher. Arthur's bark isn't harsh at all. I came quite close to having a positive thought about him.

"There's more to it than that," Marlon said.

183

"I look forward to hearing the whole list," said the woman. "But right now we need to . . . get our guest ready."

"I don't understand."

"I told you—Dr. Park isn't satisfied with the photo. The gold tip is the whole point, the diamond in the mine. That's what he's paying for."

"What are you saying?" Marlon said.

"We're FaceTiming him tonight at ten—you, me, and the diamond in the mine."

"But . . . but that could be trackable."

"Trackable?"

"In an investigation."

"Buck up, Marlon. There isn't going to be any investigation. We're talking about a missing cat."

"It's way more than that."

"But that's what it boils down to. A two- or three-day story and then everyone moves on. Unless . . . unless there's something I don't know."

"Like what?" said Marlon.

"You tell me."

"I have no secrets from you, babe."

"Then let's get started," the woman said.

"Doing what?" said Marlon.

"Restoring that gold-tipped tail to its natural state."

"How are we going to do that?"

"Here—I've brought supplies. I'll hold our little friend while you remove that paint."

"Our little friend, as you put it, is not so easy to hold. She's got a nasty streak—which I hope isn't in her DNA, by the way."

"Dr. Park doesn't care about her temperament. He cares about that tail, period."

"Fine, but I'm not going to let you hold her," Marlon said. "I'll handle it myself."

"How?"

"Mild sedation."

"We don't want her looking all droopy during the call."

"Why not, if all that matters is the tail?"

There was a long pause. What was mild sedation? I had no idea, but I didn't like the sound of it. But I did know one thing: Their nasty little friend would be extra nasty to them if only she got the chance.

At last the woman spoke. "Are we fighting?"

"Of course not. I just don't want you to get scratched again, that's all. I care about you—isn't that obvious by now?"

"Because you've given up your share of the business for me?" she said.

"No! First of all, that fight is far from over. And with the money we've got coming from Dr. Park I'll be able to keep fighting till Randa Bea says uncle. We're going to end up with the business, you and I."

Another silence. When the woman spoke again, her voice had softened. "I like the way you think," she said. "Mild sedation it is. See you tonight."

Then came another smooch. The door opened and closed. I heard the woman's footsteps crunching on gravel, getting fainter and fainter. A car started up and drove away. Inside this house, or whatever it was, Marlon groaned, like he was very worried about something. I didn't mind hearing that at all.

After that, still feeling more like myself, I explored my whole closet, top to bottom. There was no way out. I gazed at the tip of my tail and had some deep thoughts.

TWENTY

ARTHUR

NO ONE WAS HAPPY AT THE BLACKBERRY Hill Inn. Well, the guests seemed happy, although maybe not Mr. Ware in the Daffodil Room. Come to think of it, was he still here? It's hard to keep up with all the comings and goings. And also not my job, which was to . . . to . . .

What was my job? Making sure I ate all my kibble—that was part of it. And not just kibble. Eating all the food that came my way was also part of my job. I'd always tried my hardest when it came to leaving nothing in my bowl, even licking it clean every single time. What a hard worker I was!

But was that my whole job? As I went upstairs to check out the Daffodil Room, I thought and thought. What's your job, Arthur?

The answer still had not come to me when I arrived at the door with the painted daffodil on the front. I stuck my nose right into the crack under the door. Mr. Ware's scent was in the air, but not in the way it would have been if he'd been inside. Please don't ask me to explain this. You don't have the nose to understand.

I went downstairs, sipped from my water bowl in the kitchen, found a scrap on the floor by the counter where Bertha does her chopping—a good spot for scrap hunting if you're into that sort of thing, which I am. But it turned out to be onion skin, so I gave it a pass, took another sip from the water bowl, and was considering lying down by the big fridge, the coolest part of the kitchen, when I realized I was feeling a bit lonesome. I wandered into the front hall, and there was Mom at the desk and Harmony watering the tall plant that stood by the door.

I was so happy to see them! In fact, was kind of out of my mind. I ran up to Mom, so busy writing in the big book—called the guest book if I had things right—that she didn't seem to notice me. No problem! I ran over to Harmony, who turned out to be so busy watering the plant that she didn't notice me, either. Both of them had faraway looks in their eyes. Why would that be? I had no idea. But all at once I understood my job. It was to keep on running between them, faster and faster and faster and—

"Arthur!" said Harmony. "What's with you?"

Mom looked up. "I think he's reliving his moment of glory."

My moment of glory? I was a bit confused. And then it

hit me: the Frisbee contest! I won, I won, I won! I started racing around and around the front hall. Me, Arthur, the winner!

Mom started laughing, and Harmony, too. Then came something unexpected. Harmony's laughter turned to tears. Mom hurried over, drew Harmony into her arms.

"It's going to be all right, sweetheart."

"We don't know that, Mom. Something terrible is going on."

Mom opened her mouth to say something, maybe even something that would put me in the picture, but she never got to say it because that was when the front door opened. In walked a man in uniform.

He glanced around, saw Mom and Harmony, and took off his hat. They didn't see him. Was this a good time to bark? I was wondering about that when the uniformed man cleared his throat and said, "Excuse me."

There are a lot of human voices in this world, some more pleasant than others. This dude's voice was the most pleasant adult voice I'd ever heard—next to Mom's, of course. Kids' voices are the best, in my opinion. But back to the voice of this uniformed dude. How to describe it? Strong? Friendly? Polite? Cheerful? Yes, all those things and more, but I got stuck on cheerful. Whoever he was, the man in our front hall was enjoying life.

Mom and Harmony turned to him. They separated,

Harmony wiping away her tears. I barked, maybe a little late in the game.

The uniformed man shot me a real quick look. He had a brief flash of something like amusement in his eyes, but it was gone by the time he turned back to them.

"Sorry to interrupt," he said. "I'm looking for Yvette Reddy."

"That's me," Mom said. "This is my daughter, Harmony."

"Nice to meet you. My name's McKnight—Vern McKnight." He smiled. "I'm the new sheriff in town."

"I heard we had a new sheriff," said Mom. "I didn't realize you'd started already."

"Today is day one," said Sheriff McKnight. "I was hoping—foolishly—to ease into it, but that doesn't seem to be happening."

"Can I help you in some way?" Mom said.

"I got your name from Randa Bea Pruitt," the sheriff said. "She filed a report with us that a clown who worked for her over at the fair has gone missing. Cuthbert's his name—his legal name, first and last, which is all Ms. Pruitt has ever known him by. From what she told me, he was last seen taking photos at a cat beauty contest run by the fair, a contest won by your cat . . ." He flipped open a notebook. "Queenie—have I got the name right?"

"Yes," said Mom.

"And Queenie's missing, too!" said Harmony.

"Ms. Pruitt mentioned that," the sheriff said. "Which I was sorry to hear. Who knows the kind of anxiety that must be in a cat's mind at a time like this?"

Mom's eyes shifted slightly. When they returned to the sheriff, they had a different look, the look Mom has when she's paying full attention.

"Ms. Pruitt also said something about cats being switched," the sheriff went on. "Can you fill me in on that part?"

That question started up a long and very complicated back-and-forth. It was all about Queenie, Princess, that Edna woman, Cuthbert, Pamela Vance, gold paint on a white tail, and a bunch of stuff I already knew. But I hadn't known it like this! I suddenly understood the whole story. And to prove that to myself I decided to go over it all in my mind, from beginning to end. So, here goes!

Um.

Funny. The story didn't seem to be unreeling. One icy morning Mom's car wouldn't start. This was like that, just before she got to work with the jumper cables. Would jumper cables be good for cranking up my brain? I backed quickly away from that idea. Jumper cables had these sharp grippers on the ends, called alligator clips, if I'd heard Mom right. I'd seen alligators on Animal Planet, Elrod's favorite TV channel. I didn't want anything alligatorish anywhere near my brain.

Meanwhile, Sheriff McKnight was saying, "Have you got a photo of Queenie?"

"Oh, lots," said Harmony. "I'll get them." She took off, through the doorway that led to the family quarters. I heard her running up the stairs, making the very distinctive sound that two-stairs-at-a-time running makes. With my newfound speed I could have zipped right by her, taking those stairs even three or four at a time. The thought alone made me feel very good about myself.

That left me, Mom, and Sheriff McKnight in the front hall. It was one of those moments where you expect a human to say something, but neither of them did. Instead Mom went over to the plant Harmony had been watering, picked up the watering can, and put it back down in a slightly different position. Sheriff McKnight looked all around the front hall, then did it again. Were they both behaving a bit strangely? I thought so, but couldn't have said how or why or any of those other explaining things.

And then, after this strange silence, they both started speaking at once.

Sheriff McKnight said, "Nice place you've—"

Mom said, "Where were you working before—"

They both stopped speaking at the same time, and both laughed uncomfortable little laughs.

"Go ahead," Mom said.

"You first," said the sheriff.

Good grief. This was going nowhere, so it was a real relief when Harmony came running in with her phone.

"Here's a whole photo gallery I put together on Queenie." The three of them gathered at the desk, Mom looking over one of Harmony's shoulders and Sheriff McKnight over the other.

The sheriff's mouth opened. Now would come, "Oh, what a beauty," or "I've never seen such a good-looking kitty cat," or some other irritating remark. But no. Instead the sheriff said, "That's a pretty distinctive tail. The . . . what would you call it?"

"Tuft," said Mom.

"Yes," the sheriff said. "That tuft at the end—same color as her eyes. I've never seen anything like it." He glanced at Harmony. "When was the last time you had Queenie in your possession?"

"It was just after she won the contest," Harmony said.

"Where were you, exactly?" Sheriff McKnight said. "Could you draw me a diagram?"

Harmony nodded. Mom opened a drawer, took out a sheet of paper, laid it on the desk. Harmony picked up a pencil.

"Here's the circle of stools where the cats were. We followed the judge, that lady from the cat magazine—"

"Pamela Vance?" said the sheriff.

"Yeah. She led us over to the photo booth, right here.

193

It had a black curtain, like so." The tip of the pencil made real quick movements on the paper. "Then Edna handed Princess to Pamela Vance, and I gave her Queenie. Cuthbert came through the curtain with a sort of plastic box and Ms. Vance put the two cats in it. Cuthbert took the box and went back inside for the picture taking. The curtain closed."

"And then?" said the sheriff.

"Ms. Vance took us over to the snack bar, right about here. She gave us some coupons."

"Us being?"

"Me, Edna, and my brother, Bro."

I wasn't following this closely, but whoa! Hadn't I been there, too? I had a very clear memory of a pretzel morsel coming my way.

"What about Ms. Vance?" the sheriff said.

The pencil started moving again. "She went over to this table here and got busy with her phone. After a while she came over and said she was going to check on how the photo session was going. When she came back, she brought the cats. I put Queenie in the backpack and . . . but it wasn't Queenie, was it?" Harmony's face . . . hardened. Just for no time at all, but I'd never seen her face like that. "Then we went to watch the Frisbee contest."

Won by me! I waited for someone to point that out, but no one did.

"How much time went by from when the cats went

behind the curtain to when Ms. Vance brought them back?" the sheriff said.

Harmony shook her head. "I'd only be guessing."

"Guess," said the sheriff.

"Twelve minutes," Harmony said.

The sheriff gave Harmony a quick look, very direct. She gave him the same look back.

"How was Queenie behaving when you got her back?" he said.

"She was—well, I don't know, do I? Because I was paying attention to the cat I thought was Queenie. And she—Princess—seemed sleepy."

The sheriff motioned to the sheet of paper. "May I take that?"

"Sure," said Harmony.

He folded the sheet carefully and tucked it in the chest pocket of his uniform shirt.

"How old are you, Harmony?"

"Eleven."

"I'm not around kids much, but are they all like you these days?"

"In what way?" said Harmony.

The sheriff laughed. "That way, right there. And I mean it as a compliment."

"Thanks," said Harmony. "But what's going on? Are you going to find Queenie?"

Mom's eyebrows rose, like Harmony had surprised her, but Sheriff McKnight didn't seem surprised at all. "I promise to give it all I've got, Harmony." He took out his phone. "In the meantime, send me a photo or two of Queenie."

"Okay," said Harmony, and she was turning to her own phone when the door opened and Mr. Ware walked in. By Mr. Ware I mean old Mr. Ware, the slow-moving guy with the wild white hair. But he could move fast, as I knew very well. I'm the type who recalls the details about any human who tried to kick me—an easy thing to do since he was the only one—and there'd been nothing slow about that kick.

Mr. Ware saw us and paused. For a moment I thought he was going to back right out through the doorway, but he did not. Instead he came forward, moving in a creaky old man way. A low sort of growl started up in our front hall.

"Arthur?" Mom said.

I turned to her. When Mom talks, Arthur listens.

"What are you doing?" she said.

Me? Nothing. Except maybe . . . was that growling mine? It did have a catchy rumble rumble to it. How nice to have a growl like that in your back pocket! What would happen if I amped it up a bit? Couldn't hurt to try.

"Arthur!"

I put a stop to any possible growling at once.

"Sorry about that, Mr. Ware," Mom said.

"No problem," said Mr. Ware, in his old man voice,

thinner and shakier than ever. "I'm a big dog lover. Arthur's going to realize that eventually."

"Thanks for being so understanding," Mom said. "Sheriff, this is our guest Mr. Ware. Mr. Ware, meet Sheriff McKnight."

Mr. Ware shook hands with the sheriff. "Thanks for all you do," he said, his eyes glittering behind those shaggy brows.

"Haven't done anything yet," said the sheriff. "It's my first day on the job."

"Then let me wish you the best of luck." I noticed that Mr. Ware had a Band-Aid on his chin, the kind guys use to cover up shaving cuts. He slowly made his way across the hall and up the stairs to the guest room floor. Sheriff McKnight watched him until he was out of sight.

"Arthur seems like a friendly soul," he said.

"Oh, yes," said Harmony.

"So why doesn't he like Mr. Ware?"

"I have no idea," Mom said. "He's a perfectly behaved guest. Quiet, keeps to himself—you wouldn't even know he's around."

The sheriff knelt down to my level, scratched between my ears in the exact way I like. "What's on your mind, buddy?"

Good question. I gave my mind a quick search and turned up . . . bacon! Bacon was on my mind. How lucky to have a mind like mine!

197

The sheriff laughed. "If you could harness that tail wag you could cool the whole house." He rose and turned to Mom. "Has anyone ever expressed an interest in buying Queenie from you?"

"No."

"Or asked where you got her?"

"Not that I recall," Mom said. "Harmony?"

"Me either," said Harmony.

"Where *did* you get her?" the sheriff said.

"Someone left a basket of kittens outside our school," Harmony said.

"And you couldn't resist?" the sheriff said.

"I didn't even try," said Harmony.

That made the sheriff laugh again. He had a very nice laugh, a bit like some outdoor sounds I like, the river when it hits the rapids not far from our place, for example.

"Is Queenie an indoor cat?" he said.

"In theory," said Mom. "She does sneak out sometimes."

"Any idea where she goes?"

"I'm afraid she hunts birds," Mom said.

"I'd like to take a little tour of her hunting grounds," the sheriff said.

"But why?" said Mom. "We've already searched the whole property. And if she escaped from Edna's, why wouldn't she just come right to the house?"

"Good question," said the sheriff. "All I can tell you is

that in missing persons cases I like to get a feel for how the missing person lives. I don't see any reason to change things up just because it's a cat that's gone missing."

Mom gave the sheriff a look that seemed a little longish to me. Then she nodded, that quick, sure nod of Mom's, meaning her mind is made up.

"So if someone could take a few minutes to guide me around I'd be grateful," the sheriff said.

"Mind watching the desk, Harmony?" Mom said.

"I could take the sheriff on the tour," said Harmony.

"That's all right," said Mom.

She and the sheriff headed for the door. The sheriff paused and looked back at me. "And how about we deputize Arthur? Can you lay your hands on anything that has Queenie's scent?"

I missed the answer to that question. My mind was stuck on *deputize*. What did that mean? Did it have anything to do with deputy? Like in deputy sheriff? I hurried to the door, one or maybe more than one of my paws sliding out from under me, the front hall floor being slippery from all the polishing it gets. But I've got paws to spare, probably one of the reasons I'd made such a good impression on the sheriff.

TWENTY-ONE
ARTHUR

QUEENIE HAS A SMALL RUBBERY chew toy that looks like a mouse. Why would anyone give her such a thing? I once happened upon her while she was . . . toying? Was that how to put it? Why not? She'd been toying with a real mouse. I came around a corner in the old cellar—why I was there at all is a complete mystery, since it's a scary place and as a rule I avoid scary places—and there was Queenie toying with a real mouse. Not a pleasant sight and then Queenie noticed me, paused in her little game, and gave me a thoughtful look. Thoughtful for her, maybe, but rather disturbing for me, although I didn't know why at the time and still don't. I do remember making a very quick exit.

But why am I bringing this up? Oh, yes, the rubbery mouse, which Sheriff McKnight was now waving in my face.

"Can you smell Queenie, Arthur?" he said.

What a question! I smelled Queenie every single day of my life and had no need for this rubber mouse, which— which I suddenly seized! Oh, what a brilliant idea! I seized the rubber mouse right out of the sheriff's hand and took off across the field.

"Wow," said the sheriff, somewhere behind me, probably eating my dust, "what's he up to? Don't tell me he knows where she is."

"I won't," Mom said.

I glanced back. They were running to catch up, maybe even closing the distance somewhat. And possibly not actually running, but certainly walking very very fast. That was not going to cut it, my friends! After no time at all—like I was so fast I could be in two places at once!—I came to the tomato patch and, without having to think the slightest bit, came up with another idea, just as good as the idea of seizing the rubber mouse or even better. What I was going to do now was bury the thing, bury it deep among the tomato plants!

I got to work immediately. Some might say, *Oh, Arthur, it's so hot today, why not kick back, take it easy?* But that wouldn't be me! Am I the type who lies around when there's work to be done? Never! I dug and dug, front paws, back paws, all of them busy at once, faster and faster, clumps of this and that, some bearing those hairy ends, possibly called roots, flying everywhere. I was a digging machine, digging down and down, until I found myself in quite a deep hole. Wow! Probably deep enough. I dropped the rubber mouse into the bottom of the hole and started pawing all the earth back in. Paw paw, paw paw, a bit of smoothing things over—a job worth doing is worth doing well, as I'm sure you know already—and presto! All done. I gave myself a real good shake, a whole big cloud of dust rising above me, the strangest dust you've ever smelled, all tomatoey.

I looked around. Mom and Sheriff McKnight stood at the edge of the tomato patch, watching me. I knew I'd made a big impression from the way their eyes were open wide.

"What was that all about?" said the sheriff.

Mom shook her head. "Arthur seems to be . . . going through some changes."

"Like what?"

"Hard to say. When he won the Frisbee contest, I was shocked. I'd been thinking Bro—that's my son—"

"Harmony mentioned that."

"They're twins, actually," Mom said. "Do . . . do you have any kids?"

He looked away. "Afraid not."

"None of my business," Mom said. "My point was that I thought Bro was setting himself up for disappointment. You should have seen some of those practice sessions, and Arthur's never shown much in the way of athletic ability. But Bro never seemed to have any doubts. And then Arthur came through. I can't help thinking he somehow did it for Bro."

Arthur's never shown much in the way of athletic ability? What did that even mean? I couldn't figure it out, so I forgot the whole thing immediately.

The sheriff stepped into the tomato patch, stopped beside my work site, did some smoothing over of his own with the sole of his shoe. "What's their relationship like, Arthur and Queenie's?"

Mom shot the sheriff a glance. He wasn't looking her way. Her glance turned into something a bit longer. "I've thought about that," she said. "I suppose there's an underlying tension, but they've solved it—and I think deliberately—by living in different silos, at least in their heads."

The sheriff turned to her, paused a moment, and then nodded, like what she'd just said made sense. I loved Mom, but this one time I just couldn't go along with her. The only silo I knew was over at the Poulins' farm on the other side of town, which I'd seen exactly once, when we'd driven Bobby Poulin home from hockey practice after his dad got delayed. I hadn't even gotten out of the car, let alone gone into the silo. Even Mom could make a mistake. I admit that as we were driving away from the Poulins' farm I'd thought how perfect that silo would be for lifting my leg against, but the chance never came along.

And what do you know? While I was having those thoughts about the silo, I seemed to have my leg raised against a tomato plant, and the air was full of splashing sounds, soft and pleasant. There are some days that just get better and better as you go along.

The sheriff laughed.

"What's so funny?" Mom said.

"Nothing," said the sheriff. Then his gaze shifted to Mom. "Well, it's just that we—I—had a dog who liked to mark things. He marked everything in sight—hydrants, trash cans, parked cars."

"What was his name?" Mom said.

"Babe," said the sheriff.

"Interesting name for a male dog."

"I didn't choose it. My . . . my wife thought he looked just like Babe Ruth."

"Oh," said Mom.

Sheriff McKnight took a deep breath. "She died," he said. "Cancer."

"I'm sorry."

"Quite a long time ago now. Almost five years."

"But still," Mom said.

The sheriff walked away, headed toward the far end of the tomato patch, and then looked back.

"Does this tomato patch have any significance for Queenie?" he said. "Did she ever come here?"

"Not to my knowledge," Mom told him.

"I'm just wondering why Arthur would want to bury her toy here."

204

That was an easy one! I liked the soft dirt in the tomato patch and had buried many things here, for example . . . for example Mr. Ware's red clown nose! How sharp my mind was today. And when I bury something, I always remember where, and if not always at least sometimes. I trotted down the row of plants and started digging, actually not far from the spot where I'd buried the rubber mouse.

This dig took more time than the first one. Even great digging athletes, such as myself, can end up tuckered out, especially on a hot day. I dug for a bit and then just stood there, possibly with my tongue hanging out.

"Is he looking for the rubber mouse?" the sheriff said.

"He couldn't have already forgotten where he buried it," said Mom.

Of course not! And just to show the sheriff that he should always listen to Mom, I went back to work—digging, resting, digging, resting—and quite soon a foamy smell rose in the air. I stuck my muzzle into the dirt, rooted around, bumped against something round and foamy, got the round and foamy something between my teeth, and raised it up into the light.

Mom and the sheriff came closer.

"What you got there?" the sheriff said.

"Looks like a ball," said Mom.

The sheriff crouched down, held out his hand. "Can I see it?"

Well, sure, no problem. He was welcome to look at my

ball as long as he wanted. Mom, too, of course. I'm a big believer in sharing.

Sheriff McKnight reached out, as though to . . . to maybe take the ball. Taking my ball is a lot different from looking at my ball. I turned my head quite sharply, putting a bit of distance between my ball and the sheriff's hand. I'm sure you would have done the same.

The sheriff grinned, like he was having fun. Hey! Was he the playful type? Did he like the game of keep-away? What if I got going on a nice long game of keep-away, charging all around the meadow, letting the sheriff get closer and closer and then at the last moment zigzagging away from him? Wow! Did it get any better than that? Not to my way of thinking.

There was only one problem. I was all tuckered out. Yes, my friends, even world-class athletes can tire themselves out. Don't forget the midsummer heat, and the fact that I'd already dug two big holes. Charging all around the meadow? Maybe some other time. I let go of the ball.

"What a good boy!" the sheriff said.

"He's behaving very strangely," said Mom.

Did strangely mean good or bad? Had to be good. Mom was trying to say that Arthur's behavior was top notch, really couldn't be any better. My tail, not quite as tuckered out as I was, did some wagging.

Sheriff McKnight reached for the ball again but paused

just before his fingers came in contact with it. From his back pocket he took out some very thin gloves, the kind Bertha wears when she's cleaning the big black pot, and snapped them on. He picked up the ball.

First he blew off the dust. A red ball, as I already knew. He and Mom took a close look. The sheriff gave the ball a squeeze. It was very squeezable, being so foamy and spongy. The sheriff touched a tiny little patch of what looked like duct tape, stuck to the ball.

"Have you ever seen this ball before?" the sheriff said.

"I think I saw Arthur playing with it," said Mom. "But I'm not sure—there are lots of balls in his life."

"Understood," said the sheriff. "But this isn't exactly a ball. It's a clown nose."

Sometimes on hot summer days the air can suddenly get very still, and you can hear things far far away. That stillness was suddenly happening now. I heard the roar of Catastrophe Falls, which was certainly far far away, meaning the roar was very faint. But it was the first time I'd ever heard the Falls from here at our place.

Mom and the sheriff both gazed at my red ball. Then they looked at each other.

"I'd like to bring in a crew to do some digging," the sheriff said. "I could get a warrant but it would save time if you gave your permission."

"No warrant necessary," Mom said.

■ ■ ■

Not long after that we had a bunch of guys in hard hats standing around the tomato patch, plus a few gals in hard hats, too. Another gal, sitting behind the wheel of a backhoe, her long white ponytail hanging down from under her hard hat, seemed to be the crew chief.

"You're Lydia?" the sheriff said.

"Yessir."

"Let's keep the backhoe in reserve. Spades and shovels only. Take it slow and easy. And dig up the plants carefully. I want them replanted when we're done."

"Heads up," Lydia said to the crew. She turned out to have one of those commanding voices, not especially loud, but it sort of pushed at you through the air. "Spades and shovels only. Slow and easy. Careful with the plants. Any questions?"

There were no questions, maybe because the crew had now heard the whole thing twice. But who am I to question how humans work? Look at all they've done, building skyscrapers, for example. And there are other examples, although none were coming to me at the moment.

I sat and watched the digging. The crew were pretty good diggers, for humans. They dug up all sorts of stuff, most of which I remembered, such as a stuffed animal of Harmony's, a stuffed animal of Bro's, a corkscrew that I believe was Bertha's favorite, a cell phone, possibly belonging to a guest, several other gadgets I didn't know the names of, many different kinds of shoes, plus socks to go with them, various small tools of Elrod's that had been lying around, just waiting for someone to tidy things up, and a musical instrument, called a trumpet, I believe, of which I had no knowledge whatsoever, except for the tiniest smidgen. All in all, a nice little pile.

"My god," said Mom, about what, I wasn't sure.

"Want me to move in with the backhoe?" said Lydia.

The sheriff shook his head.

The crew got back to work, and after not very long at all, our tomato patch was back to the way it had been, all the plants standing in neat rows. The only problem was the pile of stuff over at one side. Were they expecting me to rebury all that? Why was it my job?

Lydia and her crew went away. The stillness of the midsummer day was gone, but I could still hear Catastrophe Falls, if anything, louder than before. Why would that be?

"What now?" Mom said.

"We've got a missing clown and a missing cat, together just before their disappearances," said Sheriff McKnight. "The two cases have to be connected. I plan on starting with the cat."

"Why?" Mom said.

"Because it's the unexpected choice."

"Unexpected to whom?"

"To whoever we're trying to scare into the open."

Mom gave the sheriff a look. He looked back at her. For a second or two, you might have thought they'd known each other for a long time.

"Sounds like a plan," Mom said.

"I'm glad to hear you say that," said the sheriff. "One other thing, Ms. Reddy."

"Yvette," said Mom.

"Okay," he said. "And I'm Vern."

"You mentioned that."

The sheriff's face turned the tiniest bit pink. He cleared his throat, one of my favorite human sounds. "Well, Yvette, I was surprised to discover that the department has no K-9 capability, something I hope to correct. So I'd like to borrow Arthur for an hour or two, if it's all right with you."

"Do you want another one of Queenie's toys?"

"This time, let's try without."

TWENTY-TWO
QUEENIE

WHY AREN'T YOU EATING? YOU'VE got to look good. So eat, you moron."

I was in the linen closet, my mind not right. So fuzzy. If I got jabbed with another needle, I really didn't know what I was going to do. And now, the jabber, Marlon, was standing over me. Although not too close. The sight of the Band-Aid on his chin brightened my day, just a little.

He pointed toward my food bowl, topped up with kibble. It was not a kibble I liked. Neither did I like the bowl. But those weren't the reasons I wouldn't take a single bite. The reason was that anything Marlon wanted me to do I would not do. Was I hungry? Possibly. But I was at peace with my decision.

Other than the Band-Aid, there was no brightness in my day. Why was I being treated like this? What had I done? I'd won a beauty contest. That was only right. Any beauty contest I entered was over from the start. Even without that golden tuft on the end of my tail, I'd—

I glanced at my tail. The tuft was golden again. A lovely sight, but when had that happened? And how? A faint smell of soap was in the air, and also a hint of oil, the kind Bertha uses in her salad dressing. I don't like soap anywhere near me, and the thought of oil on my coat is very unpleasant. But still, how nice to have my tail back to normal. Was it a sign of better things to come? I looked beyond Marlon to the closet door, closed tight.

"Eat!"

I got up and moved to the farthest corner, moving, I'm afraid, like someone else, someone who didn't glide along, or even walk smoothly. What was happening to me? What had I done? I curled up in the corner.

Marlon came forward, shoving the kibble bowl forward with his foot. He kept shoving in until it was right in my face.

"Eat!"

There I was trapped in the corner, the tips of my long— and very elegant—whiskers actually touching the rim of the bowl. The kibble—while not close to my favorite, laid out at the exact same time every day at the inn, the exact same time being the moment I needed it—actually smelled not too too terrible. I pushed the bowl away with my paw.

Marlon's voice rose. He called me horrible names. Then he shoved the bowl back in my face, this time quite hard.

"Know what I'd do to you if I could? All that's saving you is the money you're going to make for me."

Money? As though . . . what? I was going to work for Marlon? I do not work. How could anyone, even such a terrible being as him, miss such an obvious fact? I don't work for anyone, not even those I feel close to, or even . . . let's just get it out there, love. I live. I play. I have the occasional adventure. But I do not work. Why would I?

I was about to push the bowl away again when I heard the barking of a dog, not too far away. The barking of a dog is not pleasing to the ear, as you must have noticed. Dogs bark. Cats purr. Is there really anything else to be said?

But in this particular case, I was not unhappy to hear the sound. The not-too-distant bark was a bark I knew well, an odd mixture of shriek and rumble that meant only one thing. Arthur was in the neighborhood.

I pushed the bowl away with my paw.

Marlon's face went red. He drew back his foot, but at that moment came a knock, not on the door of this closet, but on another door nearby.

Marlon's kick never came. He softly lowered his foot and went still. When humans are surprised, their smells change. If it's a nice surprise, then the smell is nice, too, at least to my nose. A bad surprise means a bad smell, which was what we had now in the linen closet.

Knock knock.

Marlon stood very still, not making a sound. Arthur barked again, very loud now, right outside. Not right outside the linen closet, but outside this dwelling I was in.

Knock knock.

A man whose voice I didn't recognize called out. "Hello? Ms. Vance? You in there? Hello?"

Marlon remained very still. What was happening? Some man I didn't know was at the door, looking for Ms. Vance. Ms. Vance was someone I did know, although not well, but well enough to have learned she could be trusted, at least when it came to judging beauty. Also Arthur was out there with this unknown man. Why would that be? He should have been at home, and if not at home, then with Bro or Harmony, or Mom. Arthur was not supposed to be roaming around, and therefore lucky for him he had no interest in roaming around. The roamer was me.

What else? The only other thing I knew about this situation was that Marlon had no intention of answering that knock. Meaning the unknown man—and Arthur!—would soon be going away, possibly very soon, even this minute. I lunged forward, right over the bowl, and sank my teeth into Marlon's ankle, nice and deep.

"Arrgghh!" he cried out.

He looked at me in fury, and was about to try something really dreadful—I just knew it—when there was more knocking, much louder now. And Arthur was barking again, also much louder. A really horrible sound I loved at that moment.

"Ms. Vance? Ms. Vance?" Did I hear a doorknob being rattled? I thought so.

Marlon turned toward the closet door. "Coming!" he shouted. "Coming!"

He raised his pant leg, examined what I'd done. A good job in my opinion, although not his, as I could tell from the look he shot me, a look that promised bad things in my future. Then he moved to the closet door.

The closet door opened with one of those brass levers that get pushed down. Marlon put his hand on the brass lever. He was about to open the door. This was my chance. Was I up to it? I didn't feel too good. My mind was fuzzy, and my body had given pretty much all it had left on that lunge and bite. A glorious bite, yes, except now I was weak.

But this was my chance.

The door opened. I glimpsed a kitchen in what seemed to be some sort of cabin. Marlon stepped out of the closet. I sprang after him, headed for freedom! Without even look-ing back, Marlon slammed the door shut with his heel, right in my face. He slammed it so hard I heard a faint crack or splitting sound somewhere above, and I myself got knocked to the back of the closet, rolling and tumbling. How slow I'd become! What was wrong with me?

I heard Marlon's footsteps, moving away, but not far. "Yes?" he said.

"Sheriff McKnight," said the man outside. "Is Pamela Vance inside?"

A slight pause, and then Marlon spoke. "Pamela Vance?"

"She's the registered owner of this cabin."

"Ah," said Marlon. "I see. I'm just renting it. Through a home share. So I actually don't even know this person you're talking about."

"WOOF WOOF WOOF."

That was Arthur, no doubt about it. Some of his barks are all about confusion and most of the rest are about wanting a treat, but this one was unusual. It sounded angry. Arthur has many shortcomings but you can't call him the angry type.

"And you are?" said the sheriff. Wasn't Carstairs the sheriff? Or had he messed up in some way and lost his job, maybe after all that frightening business at Catastrophe Falls? All I knew was that this new sheriff—if that was what we were dealing with—had a much more pleasant voice.

"The renter," Marlon said.

"Your name?"

Another pause, longer than the last. "Marlon."

"Can you open the door, please, Marlon?"

"Uh, sure. Sure thing."

I heard the soft creak of the door opening. And then right away "WOOF WOOF WOOF." And more woof-woofing, yes, furious, for sure. Why Arthur would be furious was a question I couldn't answer, but I had no problem with it and wouldn't have minded if that barking went on forever.

"Hey, Arthur, easy there," the sheriff said. "He doesn't seem to like you, Marlon."

"I don't know why," Marlon said. "I'm an animal lover, big-time."

"WOOF WOOF WOOF!"

"Mind shortening up on that leash a bit?" said Marlon.

"It's short enough," said the sheriff. "C'mon, Arthur, be a good boy."

Just like that, Arthur amped his barking down to a growl. That was a surprise. How often had people asked Arthur to be a good boy with no result whatsoever? I wanted to meet this sheriff. Oh, yes, and badly. I tried to rise, but my legs weren't quite ready to do it.

"How long is your rental?" the sheriff asked.

"Oh, a week, maybe two. It's such a beautiful part of the country."

"So you're on vacation?"

"Pretty much."

"Where are you from?"

A very slight pause, and then, "Florida."

"What part?"

"The Orlando area."

"Can I see some ID?"

"ID?"

"A driver's license will do."

"But what's this about, sheriff? I thought you were look-ing for . . . for Ms. whatever her name was."

"Ms. Vance," said the sheriff. "Pamela Vance. I was told she was staying here at her cabin while the county fair's going on."

"That's strange. I've never met her, as I already told you. And she's certainly not staying here. I'm by myself."

"WOOF WOOF WOOF!"

"Arthur," said the sheriff. "Please."

"Grrrrr."

"I'm pretty busy," Marlon said, "so if that's all . . ."

"Busy?" said the sheriff. "I thought this was a vacation."

"A working vacation," Marlon said. "Work never goes away, as I'm sure you know."

"What is it you do?"

"I'm an investor."

"An investor in what?"

"Various industries."

"Such as?"

"Biotech, for one."

"Way above my pay grade," the sheriff said. "Your ID, please."

"I don't—" Marlon stopped himself. Then came a very faint rustling sound, the kind of sound that might be made by a hand sliding into a pocket. "Here you go."

A brief silence. "Marlon Pruitt," the sheriff said.

"Correct."

"An accurate photo of you. Except no Band-Aid on your chin."

"Shaving cut," Marlon said.

Another silence, except for the growling, now very low, like Arthur was tiring of it. He tired easily, of many things.

"Any relation to Randa Bea Pruitt?" the sheriff said.

"Never heard of her."

"Have I seen you before?" the sheriff said. "You look a bit familiar."

"Not that I'm aware of," Marlon said. "I know I've never seen you."

I heard a very soft smacking sound, maybe the wallet getting handed back to Marlon.

"If you happen to see Ms. Vance, tell her to call my office," the sheriff said. "Here's my card."

"Sure thing," Marlon said, "although I doubt I'll see her."

"Been to the county fair yet?" the sheriff said.

"I have no interest in fairs," said Marlon. "But you still haven't told me what this is about."

"Ms. Vance is a possible witness in an investigation."

"Ah," said Marlon.

Whoa. Back up. The sheriff's card? Was he leaving? Oh, no! I tried to rise, but again my legs wouldn't help. I needed to make a sound, to cry out. But my mouth and throat were so dry hardly any sound at all came out, just a faint little whimper I could barely hear myself.

"WOOF WOOF WOOF!"

And what was this? The sudden skittery pawing of a clumsy runner on polished floors? Was Arthur in the house? Arthur! Yes! Arthur was coming to the rescue! Skitter skitter skitter, closer and closer, a beeline toward the closet, because—he knew!

But then a kind of strangled "Eek," from Arthur, followed by a skidding sound.

"Hey!" said the sheriff. "What did you just do?"

"Grabbed the leash," said Marlon. "I don't want to pay for any damages to the property, and your dog was out of control."

"There was no need to grab so hard," the sheriff said. I heard something new in his voice, a sort of hardness, very strong and deep.

"It wasn't intentional," Marlon said. "I'm an animal lover."

"So you say."

"I'm sorry," said Marlon. "Hope I didn't hurt you, fella. Can I give him a treat?"

"Maybe some other time," said the sheriff. "Come on, Arthur."

No no no. I tried to cry out one more time, now doing a little better, but Arthur was barking again, and no human could possibly have heard me. Moments later, the sheriff and Arthur were out the door and gone. A car started up and drove away. Arthur didn't stop barking, but the sound faded away to nothing.

TWENTY-THREE
ARTHUR

SOMETHING BOTHERING YOU, ARTHUR?" said Sheriff McKnight.

What was that? I could hardly hear him, what with all the barking going on in the car. My first time in a cop car, and it was very nice, especially how I got to sit up front so I could see where we were going and what we were passing at the same time. But where else would I be sitting except for up front? Have you forgotten that I was a deputy? You're not alone. I kept forgetting, too.

"Didn't care for that guy, did you?" the sheriff said.

What guy was he talking about? I liked most guys I met just fine.

Meanwhile we were going by a mountain I'd seen before, with ski trails and chairlifts, the trails now green and the chairlifts not moving. This was Mount Ethan, where people came from all over the place to ski in winter. Lots of condos and ski houses stood at the base of the mountain, plus cabins spread out in the woods nearby, but some skiers stayed with us at the inn. Skiing guests were great.

When they came down off the mountain, they pretty much ate until bedtime and they were always happy and in the mood to share.

"You can tell a lot about a guy from how he treats a dog," the sheriff said.

No question about that, but where were we going with this? I took a good look at Sheriff McKnight. He had a strong-featured face—nothing puny about that nose or chin—but it was somehow gentle at the same time, not a combo you see every day.

He glanced at me. "Here's my advice, Arthur. Ignore the lousy people in life, don't have anything to do with them. Just enjoy the good ones."

Kind of complicated, but that part about enjoying the good ones made total sense. I was on board. Sheriff McKnight could count on me. The barking we'd had going on in our official cop car died down.

We drove into town, the part of town farthest from the river, where the inn is. The streets here are quiet, with small houses and tidy lawns. The sheriff turned onto a street I'd been on before, and not long ago.

"Tell me about Yvette, Arthur." He looked my way again and laughed. "What a world that would be, huh? You could be my confidant."

Sheriff McKnight had lost me completely. Yvette was Mom, of course, but all the rest was a mystery.

"I haven't even thought of anything like this since . . . since . . . well, it's been a long time," he said, adding to my confusion. He shook his head. "When my mom said, 'One day there'll be someone new,' and I stomped right out of her house? Like a child. But I am her child, so I guess she was looking out for me." He took a deep breath. "Wasn't nearly ready to hear it then. But now? I'm having trouble getting Yvette out of my mind. Not even sure I want to."

Mom was on his mind? What was so surprising? She was on my mind all time. What was the deal with our sheriffs? First there'd been that meanie Hunzinger, now locked up, if I'd heard right. After that came Carstairs, who'd gotten run out of town. And now this dude, not sure he wanted Mom on his mind? How were things supposed to work if you didn't have Mom on the scene, somewhere inside you?

We pulled up in front of a house with a lot of hanging plants on the porch. This was Edna's house, where Mom, Bro, Harmony, and I had gone to deliver Princess. And . . . and pick up Queenie? Wasn't that the plan? But Queenie wasn't here. I knew that very well! Queenie was back at that cabin we'd just left! The cabin where Mr. Ware answered the door, not the Mr. Ware with the wild white hair and the shaggy white eyebrows and the old man voice, but the young Mr. Ware underneath. A very bad man, or a very bad pair of men. You can tell a lot about a person by how he treats—

Whoa! And he hadn't treated me very well at all! Yanking my leash the way he had? How did he think that felt?

"Hey, Arthur, what's the matter?"

Barking had started up inside our cop car again, and the barker was me, no question. I was angry. Mr. Ware, or Marlon, or Marlon Pruitt, or whatever he was called, had Queenie back at the cabin near Mount Ethan. I thought I'd heard her there and I'd picked up her scent for sure. I even knew where to look: behind the slatted door at the back of the kitchen in that cabin.

"Arthur! C'mon now!"

Come on now? What was he talking about? It was time to pull a uey, hit the siren and the lights, and zoom back to that cabin, pedal to the metal.

Instead Sheriff McKnight cut the engine and opened his door. "If you can't zip it, you're staying in the car."

I zipped it.

We went up to the door. It opened before we got there and Edna looked out. How small she looked, especially standing next to Sheriff McKnight! She blinked once or twice, her eyes maybe a little frightened.

"Edna Fricker," the sheriff said.

"Yes?"

"My name's McKnight. I'm the new sheriff."

"I heard there was a new sheriff," Edna said.

"That's me."

"The county hasn't had much luck when it comes to sheriffs," Edna said. "If you don't mind some straight talk from a tax-paying citizen."

"Not at all," the sheriff said. "I want to hear it, from you and everyone that lives in this valley. Right now, I'd like your help in the matter of the two cats, Princess and Queenie."

"Queenie hasn't turned up yet?" Edna said.

"I'm afraid not."

"Oh, dear." She noticed me. Some humans notice me first thing, some never, and some in between. Edna turned out to be an in-betweener. "Is this your K-9 partner?" she said. "He looks so much like the Reddys' dog."

"Arthur is the Reddys' dog," the sheriff said. "He's been pressed into service as my K-9 partner for now."

K-9 partner? That was me? That was me! What a roll I was on! Was it time to get busy and start arresting people? Any reason not to begin with Edna? She was right here, after all, easy pickins. I awaited the go signal from my law enforcement partner. We were going to enforce the law like it had never been enforced before.

Meanwhile there'd been some back and forth that I'd missed and now we were in Edna's kitchen and Edna was pouring iced tea into two tall glasses. There was only one door to the kitchen. I plunked myself square in the doorway, sitting up tall. Anyone wanting in or out had to go through ol' Arthur. Want to try me, Edna? Huh? Huh? Huh?

They drank tea and talked about all sorts of stuff I'd heard before. The beauty contest, Pamela Vance, Cuthbert the clown, now missing. Whoa! Cuthbert was missing? Had I already known that? It sounded important. Now that I was in law enforcement, I should probably pay attention when folks went missing. And I was just about to pay attention—pay attention and big-time!—when I noticed Princess curled up on what looked like a very comfy down pillow in the corner. Duck down, by the way—anything ducky being one of the easiest smells out there. At the same time I saw her she saw me.

We gazed at each other. I sent one single and very clear message. *Princess, you're now looking at a law enforcement officer. Mess with me and you're toast.* I felt huge inside, huge and getting huger.

Princess rose, no doubt pretty intimidated by my stare. Now she was about to go slink away and hide behind the fridge or the stove. I realized that I was going to have to get used to lots of slinkers from now on, slinkers slinking away from Deputy Arthur.

Princess stretched in a slinky way and headed for

227

the . . . Except she didn't head for the fridge or the stove, instead made her way over to me. Was she planning to make a run for it? Good luck with that, my little catty outlaw. Any idea what's going to happen to you if you even try? I was still thinking of terrible things that would happen to her when she circled around and sort of backed into the space between my front paws, wriggling around a bit to make herself comfortable.

Sheriff McKnight glanced at us over the rim of his glass. "Princess seems to have a friendly disposition."

"Very much so," said Edna. "Unlike . . . unlike the actual winner of the so-called competition."

"You're talking about Queenie?"

"I'm not in the habit of talking negatively about anyone."

"Of course not," the sheriff said. He sipped his iced tea. "Do you have any reason to think the competition was fixed?"

"Goodness, no. I wouldn't ever want to suggest such a thing." Edna stirred a spoonful of sugar into her glass. "Even if it was sticking out like a sore thumb."

"Very commendable of you." The sheriff rose. "Now I'd like to take a look at the screen Queenie tore through."

"Certainly," said Edna. "I haven't had it repaired yet— a long waiting list down at the hardware store this time of year."

Edna led us out of the kitchen through . . . through

another door, one I possibly hadn't noticed, surely not an important door. Down a hall we went, Edna first, then the sheriff, followed by me and Princess, her tail sort of curling into my coat. At that moment I got hit by a strange thought: I preferred Queenie. And it wasn't even close.

We entered a small den with lots of musty quilts around. Edna pointed out the open window, the big hole in the screen, and hole-shaped piece of screen lying on the floor.

Sheriff McKnight knelt and examined the piece of screen, running the edges through his hands. Without looking up, he said, "Queenie didn't break out."

"I don't understand," Edna said.

"This piece was cut out with metal shears," the sheriff said. "Someone broke in and grabbed her."

Edna put her hand to her chest. "Someone broke into my house?"

The sheriff nodded.

"Do you think they'll come back?"

"No," the sheriff said. "But I'd get that screen fixed as soon as you can and in the meantime keep the window closed and locked."

"Gracious." Edna went the window, closed, and locked it. She turned to the sheriff. "I was thinking of asking the Reddys to pay for the repair."

"Were you?"

"It being their cat and all."

The sheriff said nothing.

"Probably not appropriate," Edna said. "What with this new development."

The sheriff nodded a very small nod.

Edna tested the window, made sure it was locked up tight. She gazed outside. "Who would do such a thing?"

"We're going to find out," the sheriff said. By *we*, he meant me and him, just in case you missed that. We were the law in this here county.

TWENTY-FOUR
ARTHUR

WE DROVE UP TO MY PLACE, THE Blackberry Hill Inn, in our cop car, me in the shotgun seat, where deputies sat, and Sheriff McKnight in the sheriff's spot, behind the wheel. We got out, both from his side, possibly a bit of a crowded moment, but I couldn't wait to be home, so who could blame me?

The sheriff stood by the car door, maybe about to hop back in and drive off to the station. Should I be checking into the station, too? Was it possible I had my own snack supply, just waiting there? I was wondering about that when the sheriff said, "How about I walk you to the door?"

Fine with me. We walked up the brick path together. "You did good, Arthur," he said.

How nice of him! I'd had a notion that I'd done good—especially for my very first day on the job—but now it was for sure. True, we hadn't actually cuffed anybody yet and thrown them in the hoosegow, but we'd let Edna Fricker know what was what in a way she wouldn't soon forget!

She'd probably be spreading the news to all her buddies in the knitting world: There's a new sheriff running the county and he's got a deputy you don't want to mess with.

The sheriff opened my front door and we went inside. Harmony ran out from behind the desk.

"Have you found Queenie?"

"Not yet," the sheriff said. "Is your mom around?"

"She went into town," Harmony said. "But did you find out anything? Do you have any leads?"

Sheriff McKnight looked a little surprised by the question. So was I. What were leads, exactly? I knew *lead* was another way of saying *leash*. We hadn't found any leashes, me and the sheriff, and besides, Queenie didn't have a leash. I got a little confused.

"We did learn something," the sheriff said. "I was hoping to tell your mom."

"You can tell me, sheriff," said Harmony. "I'll pass it on."

"Of course," said the sheriff. "Should have thought of that myself. The main discovery is that Queenie didn't escape from Edna's place. Someone broke in and took her."

"I wondered about that," Harmony said.

"You did?" said the sheriff.

Harmony gave him one of her clear-eyed looks, plus a little nod.

"What made you think of it?" the sheriff said.

"The hole in the screen was so big," Harmony said.

"Why would Queenie need to waste time with that? She can squeeze through hardly any hole at all. Plus, the edges were so straight on the cut-out piece. Isn't that a human thing?"

Sheriff McKnight took out his notebook. "Mind if I steal that?"

"Steal what?"

"The part about straight edges being a human thing." The sheriff wrote in his notebook and put it away. "Here's the kind of question you'll hate. I know I hated it when I was a kid, but—any idea what you want be when you grow up?"

"Bro and I both want to be pro hockey players."

The sheriff laughed. "I said the exact same thing when I was—how old are you? Eleven?"

"Yeah."

"When I was your age. How much fun would that be—flying all around the country, suiting up every night in front of thousands of crazy fans, playing with and against the very best!"

Harmony grinned.

"But," the sheriff said "if it doesn't work out, consider law enforcement."

Good advice. Maybe I could . . . could take Harmony under my wing, as humans say, although of course I don't have wings. At that very moment I got itchy in the exact places where my wings would be attached if I had them. Both of those places were suddenly very itchy and also very hard to scratch. There was really only one way to do it. I lay on my back and wriggled around wildly, mouth open, tongue out and flopping all around. You'd have done the same.

"In a way," the sheriff said, "we're better off. A lost cat wandering off on her own can very soon be a dead cat. A stolen cat is more likely to be alive."

"But stealing our cat?" Harmony said. "Who would do such an awful thing?"

"Someone who wanted Queenie," said the sheriff.

"Why?"

"Hard to say. One thing for sure—Queenie's a very beautiful cat."

"So this is like stealing one of those famous paintings that can never be sold?" Harmony said. "Just so you can have it?"

The sheriff gave her a long look. "That's one possibility."

He gazed down at me. By that time, I'd gotten rid of the itchiness from the wings I didn't have, and was sort of just lying there, paws up in the air and my tongue hanging out the side of my mouth in a comfortable manner. In short, I was nice and relaxed.

"Has Queenie ever had kittens?" the sheriff said.

Harmony shook her head. "She's been fixed."

"That takes care of that idea," the sheriff said.

"What idea?"

"That our culprit is some sort of renegade cat breeder."

And now Harmony was giving the sheriff the same sort of long look he'd given her, like . . . like they were thinking together. Could that really happen?

"So what else is left?" she said.

"I don't know," said the sheriff. "But that's all right. Searching for why when it comes to crime is just one way to go. For example, we could start with—"

"Who," Harmony interrupted.

"You got it," said Sheriff McKnight. "Any ideas?"

Harmony shook her head. What was this about? Queenie? Queenie and where she was? Didn't we already know that? Or . . . or was it just me? Uh-oh.

TWENTY-FIVE

QUEENIE

DARKNESS.

Then the linen closet light flashed on. The door opened and Marlon Pruitt, my enemy, stepped inside. There are many kinds of human sweat, some of them—like the sweat just after a hard workout—smelling not too bad. Then there's nervous sweat, very unpleasant. You want to keep your distance from it. As Marlon came in, the closet filled with the odor of nervous human sweat. I couldn't keep my distance from it. Marlon closed the door after him. There was nowhere to go.

But . . . but when he closed the door, it made that same faint cracking sound high up that it had made that last time, when Marlon had slammed the door right in my face. That was something to think about, except there was no time. On one of Marlon's hands was a thick, heavy glove that reached almost to his elbow. Elrod wore gloves just like it for chain-saw work. In his other hand, Marlon held a long, shiny needle. He came toward me, both hands extended. Of all the outside things about a human, the most interesting is the hand. Sometimes I even think of the hand as a very small person.

So now it was three against one.

"I had no idea you'd be so difficult," Marlon said. "Bottom line—I'm not going to have my plans upset by some dumb animal, no matter how beautiful in the eyes of some."

Had I heard right? Was he suggesting that I was a dumb animal? The man was deranged.

He took another step. "Now we're going to take another picture of you, focusing on that gold-tipped tail that's got Dr. Park so excited. This has to be a good picture so I'll need you to be nice and relaxed." He gestured with the long shiny needle. "This will help you get in the right mood."

Oh really? What I needed for getting into the right mood was the complete absence of him. I needed my freedom! I needed to be home!

And another step. "This can be easy," he said, "or it can be hard. Up to you. But it's going to happen and there's nothing you can do about it."

Marlon smiled. I'd seen nasty smiles once or twice, but never one as nasty as this, like some monster was inside him, almost ready to climb out. He raised the needle up high. The syringe part held some sort of cloudy liquid. I did not want that cloudy liquid anywhere near me, and certainly not in my body. Oh, yes, I knew what was going on. Bertha and I sometimes watch the little TV on the kitchen counter when she takes a break. I've seen all kinds of things on that little TV, although I don't pay close attention. Except for the fishing shows, which I can't take my eyes off for some reason.

But the point was I had no intention of letting that needle come any closer. Now it quivered slightly and a single drop of the cloudy liquid appeared at the tip of the needle and hung there. The sight maddened me. I sprang up—not with my usual speed, oh, far from it—aiming for Marlon's upper arm, nowhere near the needle, where I would sink my teeth in deep, making him cry out, drop the needle, and collapse moaning to the floor. I had it all thought out.

But none of it happened. Instead, while I was still in midair, that other hand, the one wearing the chain-saw glove, shot out and grabbed me, circling tight around my neck. I writhed around in Marlon's grip, I hissed, I screamed, I thrashed, but all of that in the air, my claws and teeth scratching and biting at nothing,

Marlon smiled that smile again. "Meow," he said. The needle came flashing down. What happened right after that? I don't know. But I was aware of the door opening and closing—closing once more with that faint creak or splintering, up high.

And then nothing.

■　■　■

Darkness.

Alone.

Alone in the closet. Some things came back to me and some did not. But have you ever noticed that once in a while you wake up knowing something you didn't know when you went to sleep?

This was what I knew: I had to climb that slatted door.

Up and at 'em, Queenie! That's what Bertha says when she sets out my morning cream, fresh cream she pours into the special china saucer known as Queenie's saucer. I missed my saucer. I missed my cream. And missed Bertha as well, I suppose I should add. But most of all I missed my cream. I was weak from lack of cream.

Up and at 'em, Queenie. I rose, all wobbly, and sank right back down. I rose once more, still wobbly, and made my way across the closet floor. The smell of nervous human sweat lingered in the air. I . . . I was going to die in this closet. I had to get out.

Faint light—as though from a lamp in a room not too far away—shone dimly through the spaces between the slats. It's hard to imagine anything easier to climb than a slatted door. On a normal day for a normal Queenie. But this was not a normal day and I was not a normal Queenie. Although I was still the most beautiful cat in the county. That hadn't changed and never would. How could it if life made sense? Fact one: Queenie, the most beautiful cat in the county. Or was it the state? Or the whole country? My mind was a bit confused, as yours would be, too, if you were in a situation with a bad person, a needle, and cloudy liquid. Just the thought of it made me want to puke. I puked, and felt a little better. I placed a front paw on the lowest slat in the door.

Climbing is not something I have to think about. I just do it. If I want to go up—say onto a tree branch—I simply go up. If I want to go down, I simply go down. I never think about any of my movements. My body handles them on its own, thank you very much. But now, with one front paw on the lowest slat, I found myself thinking: What next?

My other front paw, perhaps? I tried that. It seemed to work. How about getting a back paw involved? I tried that, too, and ended up losing my balance and sinking back down to the floor. And while I was down on the floor, defeated, as you might say—although I never would—two things happened that made me try again, which I would have done anyway. Please remember that when you think of me.

First, I heard a phone ringing and Marlon saying, "Pictures turned out great. Yes, I got the gold tip. Don't you trust me, babe? See you soon." Click.

Second, lying on my back the way I was and gazing upward, I understood where that cracking sound was coming from. One of the slats—almost at the very top—had split down the middle. Not split totally: The slat was still sort of in one piece, but now it sagged in the middle, so the gap between that slat and the slat above was a little bigger. Here's something you should know about me: I can squeeze through very very small spaces.

I rose again. And again I placed a front paw on the lowest slat in the door. Then—oh, thank you, my lovely body!—then my body took over and carried me straight up the door, slat after slat whizzing by, the whole trip effortless! I stuck my head through the gap—a very narrow gap, by the way, much narrower than it appeared from below, meaning that at first just my nose was poking out the other side—and then my body flowed through, no other way to describe it, simply an easy flow from inside that horrible closet to outside, and on down to the kitchen floor, all of this in total silence, Queenie-style.

I looked around the kitchen. A small, simple cabin-in-the-woods-type kitchen, of no particular interest. But what was this? A mouse? Oh, but yes, a fat mouse sitting up right in the middle of the floor, nibbling lazily on a chunk of what smelled like cheddar cheese. Ordinarily I would . . .

But this was not an ordinary time. And so I made the most difficult decision of my life, and did the most difficult thing. I ignored that fat mouse completely, didn't give him a second look. I allowed him to sit right there in the middle of the floor, munching away, oblivious to the fact that if I so desired, I could—

Better to leave it right there. I walked out of the kitchen, partly because I saw no obvious way to the outdoors and partly to get away from temptation. The only door from the kitchen led into a hall lined with open lockers filled with skis, boots, poles. The hall was dimly lit, the only light coming from an open doorway to one side. At the far end of the hall stood the front door, a front door with a letter slot. Letter slots are narrow—I'd never even tried one—but this seemed wider than most. I headed for the letter slot, glancing into the open doorway on one side as I went by.

And there, on a couch and gazing at his phone, sat Marlon. Why would he look up at that moment? I hadn't made a sound. But he did look up. Our eyes met. He shouted something nasty and leaped to his feet, so fast. I tore off down the hall, sort of fast, although not my fastest on account of my still not feeling that good. I reached the door, leaped up to the letter slot, stuck a paw inside, wriggled, and struggled. But got nowhere. Meanwhile Marlon's running feet pounded down the hall, closer and closer. I twisted around to face him, bared my teeth, which was when I saw he had a fireplace poker in his hand. I jumped to one side, very quick, but he was quick, too. He didn't swing that poker, instead poked it into my side and pressed hard, pinning me to the floor. I wriggled and struggled and—

And that was when the front door opened from the outside. Marlon turned his head to look. It was Pamela Vance.

"Hi, Marlon, are we all—"

"Shut the door!" he screamed.

But in taking his eye off me, he'd let the poker slip, and now I squirmed free. Ms. Vance's eyes widened. Half in the cabin and half out, she pivoted, grabbed the edge of the door, tried to slam it closed. Too late! I shot through the narrowing gap and into the night! Freedom!

"Oh my god! How could you let that happen?"

"I let it happen?"

"Who else was in charge of the cat?"

The furious voices of Marlon and Pamela rose behind me, something about their anger making them sound similar, like they were almost one person. One very bad person, and now after me. I glanced back and saw their running silhouettes, framed in the light of the cabin doorway, and heard their running feet. I, too, was running, but silently of course, across a small lawn and into the woods. Ah, the woods. The woods, the night, and me. I was safe in the woods, and the deeper I got the safer I'd—

A beam of light came sweeping my way, then paused, with me right in it.

"There she is!"

Not good. I dodged to one side, out of the beam. It swept back and forth, missing me and missing me again, but their drumming footsteps came closer and closer. What to do? My mind was so tired and fuzzy. Then my body—oh, thank you, lovely body—took charge and the next thing I knew I was climbing up the nearest tree, maybe not with my usual speed or grace, but up up up and out almost to the end of a high branch. Down below the beam swept back and forth, and suddenly Marlon and Pamela appeared. She ran very fast, a flashlight in her hand, and Marlon trailed slightly behind, panting heavily. I stayed right where I was, still and silent. They passed directly under me, so intense I could feel it, like an intensity cloud rising up.

Their footsteps faded away, and the yellow cone of the flashlight grew dimmer and dimmer and finally winked out. I waited. The moon came out. I waited some more. An owl hooted. Once I'd had an encounter with an owl, and once was enough. I crept down from the tree and headed for home. Where was home? I wasn't sure. But my body would know.

The moon is special to me. Of all the beauties of the night, the moon is the most beautiful, so you can understand why I feel about the moon as I do. Like me, the moon moves with a silent grace. I followed it now as it peeped in and out of view through the treetops. After what might have been a long time, or almost none at all, I crossed a dirt road that seemed familiar. A long white-painted fence rail ran along the side, shining in the moonlight. Mom was a big believer in fresh paint. I walked under the rail and into a meadow I knew very well. Not far away rose the old barn, and much closer stood the wishing well. Not long after Dad had gone away with Lilah Fairbanks, Mom and I had paid a night visit to the well. She held a silver coin in her hand and stood before the well for a long long time. Then she sighed, pocketed the coin, and we turned for home.

"I was going to wish bad things for him, Queenie," she said. "But he's the father of my children."

That was a very strange night. And more strangeness was happening now. A person—not Mom—was standing by the well. This person was very busy, uncoiling a long rope ladder. The moonlight shone on his face. It was Maxie Millipat.

TWENTY-SIX

ARTHUR

I CAN SLEEP JUST ABOUT ANYWHERE, but most nights I prefer Bro's room. I start on the floor, where there is almost always a comfy pile of clothes, some dirty, some clean, but I end up on the bed. Once I'm on the bed, I usually start at the bottom, but I often find myself at the top, sharing Bro's pillow, or, if I get the feeling he doesn't really care all that much about the pillow, taking it for myself.

That was what we had going on the night after my first day in law enforcement. Law enforcement turned out to be extremely tiring. I was so tired I didn't really need to wriggle around on the pillow to get comfortable, but I did anyway. Why? Because in law enforcement we did things right, as I'd learned from watching the sheriff. For example, his pants had a neat crease. We were neat-crease types in law enforcement, and if I was a pants wearer you would have been amazed by the neatness of my creases. Since I wasn't a pants wearer, I did the next best thing, which was wriggling around on the pillow. I wriggled, wriggled, and wriggled some more. How deliciously sleepy I was, but the wriggling made the feeling even more delicious, so I kept doing it, wriggling and wriggling and—

"Arthur, cool it."

That was Bro, muttering something, his voice thick with sleep, that I interpreted as *cool it*, but maybe he was saying something else, like *Arthur! Do whatever deputies have to do!*

So I wriggled a bit more.

"Arthur!"

Aha. Right the first time. Wow. This really was my day. I put a stop to the wriggling, rolled over, and fell into a deep sleep at once.

Have you ever noticed that dreamtime can be connected to what goes on in the rest of your life? Actually I have not, but something like that was happening in my dreams now, my head on the pillow, not far from Bro's. I could even feel his breath on my fur, and smell it, of course. Bro's breath had a nice minty smell, which came from chewing minty gum. Not that he was chewing gum at the moment. His wad of gum was stuck to the headboard, ready to be popped back into his mouth first thing in the morning.

But we're way off track. Back on the track I was . . . I was . . . having thoughts about dreams! Got it! Whew. That was a close one. I was getting to the subject of pants, and how I never wore them, creased or not. What I do wear is my collar. There are two silver tags on it, one with my name—Arthur!—and the other . . . well, I'm not sure what's on the other tag. It's not important. What's important is that in my dream Sheriff McKnight was crouching in front of me and hooking something else to my collar, something shiny and golden, namely a deputy badge. What a great dream! I kept it right there, with me, the sheriff, and my badge, kept it and kept it until I began to hear a sound that bothered me.

This sound came through our open window, which faced the toolshed and beyond it the meadow, and was very faint and distant. I opened my eyes. I hear better with my eyes open. What's with that? Had to be some reason I would never figure out, so I stopped thinking about it at once. You can always rely on me for that sort of thing. With my eyes open, I now heard an oddity about the sound. Not only was it far away, but also it had a tiny hollowness or echo or something, like it was coming out of a cave. I'd had an experience with a cave once, very scary.

I rose, eased down off the bed, got a paw caught in one of Bro's sneakers, shook it off, and went to the window. I pressed my nose against the screen and felt the warm night air. The moon was up and everything looked nice and peaceful. Then the sound came again, not nice and peaceful at all. Far away, echoey, faint, yes, but a human voice, crying out. I came very close to recognizing that voice, which was pretty amazing, although that's the kind of ability you find in the law enforcement community. The voice faded away. I stayed where I was. An owl hooted from over in the woods. Silence. Well, not a complete silence. I could actually hear the very soft roar of Catastrophe Falls. After a while the wind rose up and took the sound of Catastrophe Falls away. Around the same time, the human cry started up again, no closer but now a little stronger, getting pushed by the wind.

I went over to the bed. Moonlight shone on Bro's face. Kids need their sleep. That's something Elrod says all the time. "When I was a kid I slept twelve hours straight, every night, rain or shine." I believed him completely. Even now he was a great napper. Not in my league, of course.

But I didn't want to wake Bro. His face was so calm, and somehow in the moonlight he looked younger than he was. Part of my job was taking care of him. Then the cry came again. I made a low, rumbly sound. No reaction from Bro. I bumped his shoulder with my muzzle. He rolled over the other way. I barked, not loud, just a bark between him and me. He rolled back over and opened his eyes.

"Arthur? What is it?"

I started wagging my tail, the only idea that came to mind.

"Go back to sleep." He closed his eyes.

I barked again, louder this time.

Bro's eyes snapped open.

"You have to go outside?"

No! Well, yes, but not for that. I barked again, maybe a little louder than I'd meant to.

"Arthur! You're gonna wake up the whole house!"

The door opened and Harmony came in. She wore white pj's—Bro wore sweatpants and a torn T-shirt—and almost looked like a stone statue in the moonlight.

"What's going on?" she said.

"Arthur's restless," said Bro. "I think he wants to go out."

"I thought you walked him before bed."

"I did. But you know how he sometimes doesn't pee when he's supposed to and just holds on for later."

A discussion about my peeing habits started up. Ordinarily I would have found that very interesting—anything involving peeing is interesting, as I'm sure you know. But the human cry came again, still as distant as before yet much louder. I glanced at Harmony and Bro. They hadn't heard it? How was that possible?

I went to the window and pressed my nose to the screen again. The peeing discussion went on and on. I barked, an impatient sort of bark I couldn't have kept inside even if the thought had occurred to me.

"For god's sake!" Harmony said.

They came over and stood beside me.

"Maybe there's a fox out there," Bro said.

They gazed into the night.

"I don't see anything," Harmony said. "But . . . but maybe I hear something."

"What kind of something?" said Bro.

"Shh. Listen."

They both turned an ear toward the screen. They were trying so hard! I loved Harmony and Bro. They always tried hard at everything. Trying hard was one of Mom's big beliefs. But those little ears! Sometimes trying hard is not enough.

"Hear anything?" Harmony whispered.

"Just you whispering," said Bro.

She glared at him, was about to say something, and then went still.

"Hear that?" she said, her whisper even fainter than before.

"Nope," said Bro.

"Listen."

They listened. The distant human cries rose, faded, rose again.

"Maybe," Bro said. "It sounds kind of like a horse. Over in the apple orchard."

"We don't have a horse."

"Then what is it?"

"There's only one way to find out."

Bro rose, somehow slipping on his sneakers in the same movement.

"What about Mom?" Harmony said.

"Let her sleep."

Harmony thought about that.

"C'mon, Harm. Time to step it up. We're almost twelve years old."

Harmony nodded. "I'll bring my phone." She looked at me. "Super quiet now, Arthur."

Super quietly we headed out of Bro's room, down the stairs, and out the side door. I didn't hear a thing. Well, actually I heard plenty, but just pretended I didn't. Soon we crossed the lawn and entered the meadow, me in the lead, following those human cries. They came and went, but when they came, the sound was closer, and getting closer with every step. The moonlight made it easy to find our way, and Harmony and Bro were also wearing their headband lights. Headband lights were a bit scary and the sight of them always got me barking, but would that have been super quiet? I moved on in silence, a deputy on the job for the county.

We sped through the night, following the cries to the apple orchard, where the moonlight turned all the apples silver. It turned out the cries weren't coming from the apple orchard, but from somewhere beyond, somewhere over thataway, in the direction of the old wishing well. Some memory, perhaps recent, about the wishing well stirred in my mind, but it got smothered by that other memory, of my visit with Mom at the end of the whole Lilah Fairbanks episode. I didn't blame myself one little bit. You can only remember so much in this life.

Meanwhile the cries had gone silent. We headed for the wishing well anyway. There was nothing else in this direction except the empty meadow, sloping all the way down to the river. The kids came to a sudden stop.

Harmony pointed toward the well. "Bro?"

Something white seemed to be poised on the low wall of the well, something very still and I suppose I should add beautiful.

"It's Queenie!" Harmony said.

I was pretty sure it was not. I don't mean the white figure. That was Queenie, all right. I mean whoever had been crying those cries. No time to think about that because now the three of us were on a dead run.

"Queenie! Queenie! Queenie!"

Slowly Queenie turned her head in our direction, those golden eyes now not golden but like two tiny moons. Did she come running to us, beside herself with happiness? Ha! Instead we did the running, Harmony scooping Queenie into her arms as soon as we reached the well and hugging her tight, while Bro patted her, and I just stood there waiting for this little meet and greet to end.

It might have gone on forever, but then, from down in the well, came that human cry. "Help! Help me! I'm going to die!"

TWENTY-SEVEN

QUEENIE

A VERY GOOD MOMENT IN MY LIFE, THIS reunion with my family, now spoiled. Harmony and Bro rushed to the edge of the well, peered down, their headlamps probing the darkness below.

"Oh my god!" Harmony said.

"Maxie?" said Bro.

"Help! Help!"

"Maxie?" said Harmony. "What are you doing down there?"

"GET ME OUT OF HERE!"

If you think much about humans—which I do not—you come to the conclusion that there are good ones and bad ones. Mom, for example, is a good one, the best I've ever encountered. Marlon Pruitt was a bad one, as bad as they get. I would have placed Maxie Millipat in the good category if he'd ever actually crossed my mind, but on this particular night I wasn't so sure.

Let's start with how I'd first seen him as I'd come out of the woods, standing by the well and fussing over a rope ladder. Good or bad? After a while, when he'd gotten it all straightened out, he reached into a backpack and took out a wooden mallet and some tent pegs with hooked tops, just like the tent pegs we have at home. I know because once I'd been taken on a family camping trip. Never again, by the way. Maxie then tapped the tent pegs into the top rope strand, gave the ladder a few tugs to make sure things were firmly planted, and put on a forehead lamp of his own. After that, he tossed the other end of the ladder into the wishing well. Then he swung one leg over the low circular wall of the well, grabbed on to the rope ladder, and started down. Almost at once, the pegged-down part of the ladder popped up out of the ground, the whole shebang getting yanked toward the well, up and over the lip, and down the other side, like the well had decided to swallow the ladder, with Maxie on it.

A troubling image. Perhaps I should have kept it to myself. After that came the sound of a fairly distant splash, followed by watery thrashing, and finally some screaming—calls for help, that sort of thing. The beam of his headlamp stabbed wildly up into the night sky and then went out. The volume of Maxie's screaming rose a notch or two.

Maxie's screams were rather unpleasant, so I got ready to put him in the bad category. On the other side of the argument we had the fact that he was some sort of friend of the twins, which would make him good. I climbed onto the lip of the well and gazed down, but it was too dark down there for even me to see. Meanwhile I was thirsty, tired, and hungry, too much of all those things. So I just sat there in the moonlight, maybe not at my best, but free. Free and on my own land.

Sometime after that, Harmony, Bro, and . . . and Arthur—I suppose I have to include him—had finally found me. No doubt they hadn't rested since my disappearance and had been searching for me the whole time, but couldn't they have been quicker? Still, I welcomed them. I was planning to let them cuddle me to their hearts' content, except we had hardly gotten started when Maxie piped up from down in the well. Interrupting my big moment, if you see what I mean.

So: Maxie bad.

Meanwhile, the night had turned very noisy.

"How did you get down there in the first place?"

"GET ME OUT OF HERE!"

"Did you just dive in?"

"GET ME OUT OF HERE!"

"With what?"

"A ROPE!"

"We don't have a rope."

"THEN GO GET ONE!"

And now Maxie began to cry, a horrible sound. Harmony

turned to Bro. "Isn't there a coil of rope on the wall in the old barn?"

Without a word, Bro ran off toward the old barn. Harmony leaned over the lip of the well. "Don't worry, Maxie. Bro's gone for a rope."

"It's so bad, Harmony," Maxie sobbed.

"Just hang on," said Harmony. "Are you treading water?"

"No, no. It's worse than that."

"What do you mean?"

"JUST GET ME OUT OF HERE!"

"Everything's going to be all right."

Down in the well, Maxie whimpered and said nothing. Harmony reached out and stroked my back. It felt nice. I let her keep doing it.

"Where have you been, Queenie?" she whispered.

Nowhere I wanted to think about ever again. I preferred to simply be stroked for the time being, although a nice late dinner and a bowl of fresh cream would hit the spot. Any reason we couldn't get going? I'd tired of Maxie and his situation. Everyone said he was brilliant. I was sure he'd figure it out eventually. To give Harmony the hint, I eased myself off the top of the well and took a step or two toward home, just the roof visible from where we were, the shingles the color of the moon. But at that moment, Bro came running up, a big coil of rope over his shoulder.

I'm the type who really needs no one, as I'm sure you've

noticed by now. And when someone of that type decides it's time for a nice late dinner and a bowl of fresh cream— served in Queenie's special saucer, of course—then that someone doesn't hesitate to get the show on the road, waiting for no one. Yet in this case our particular someone was in fact hesitating. Why?

Bro lowered the free end of the rope into the well, letting it uncoil slowly from his shoulder.

"Can you see it, Maxie?" he called down.

"Yeah," said Maxie in a weak voice.

"Then grab on and pull yourself up."

"How?"

"Huh?" said Bro. "Just climb."

"CLIMB HOW?"

"Plant your feet on the side of the well," Harmony called down. "Then go hand over hand on the rope and walk up at the same time, small steps."

I heard Maxie muttering down below. ". . . feet on wall . . . hand over . . . small steps . . ." Then came a grunt or two, followed by a sudden cry, a splash, and a scream that hurt my ears. My only thought was: Can we go home now?

Bro and Harmony looked at each other.

"Time to get Mom," Harmony said.

"Uh, let's try one more thing," Bro said.

Harmony's gaze stayed on him a little longer. Then she nodded. Bro pulled the rope up out of the well, took it to the nearest tree, wrapped it around the trunk, and began tying a knot. "Rabbit comes out of his hole, goes around the tree twice, around the hole, and back in the hole," he said as he worked. This was a bit confusing since there was no rabbit to be seen, heard, or smelled in the vicinity.

Bro rose and came back, wrapping the free end of the rope around his waist.

"And your plan is?" Harmony said.

"Rappel down," said Bro.

"I must have missed when you learned how to do that," she said.

"Saw it on TV," he told her. Then he stepped up onto the top of the well, turned so he was facing out, got the rope nice and taut, and began to lower himself down. Harmony moved closer and peered down. Since by that time I was on her shoulder, I had a good view, although mostly what we saw was the glare of Bro's headlamp. I could feel the fear inside Harmony. There was lots of it, but she didn't say a word.

Using the rope and his feet, which must have been what rappelling was about, Bro went down and down. Then came a faint splash, and the headlamp beam swept back and forth over the wet stone of the well. I glimpsed Bro way way down there, standing in water up to his chest, and Maxie soaking wet and shivering whenever the beam passed over him.

"Maxie," Bro said. "Just breathe."

260

"I can't."

"Sure you can," Bro said. "Just breathe and get on my back."

"I can't."

"Try."

"But—"

"Don't think, Maxie. Get on my back."

Bro's headlamp blinked out. The inside of the well went black, down beyond the moonlight.

"Oh my god!" Maxie cried.

"Bro?" said Harmony.

"Battery died," Bro called up. "We're good. Ready, Maxie? On two."

"On two what?" said Maxie.

"Hang on," Bro said.

The rope went very taut. Bro grunted once or twice, quite softly. At the same time he seemed to be humming under his breath. Was that possible? I turned to Harmony, her face so close. It wore an expression I'd never seen on it before. She was scared but also proud of her brother, no doubt about that.

And now he rose up into the moonlight, hand over hand on the rope, bare feet—he'd lost his sneakers—walking up the side of the wall, and all this with Maxie on his back, his arms wrapped around Bro's chest. Up up up they came and as they approached the top, Harmony set me on the ground, turned, and grabbed Maxie's shoulders with

261

both hands, and hauled him out of the well. Bro scrambled up and then there we all were, standing by the wishing well in the moonlight. Well, except for Arthur, still here, in a manner of speaking, but now lying down and fast asleep, tongue hanging out to the side in his usual way.

Harmony patted Bro on the back. "My Bro," she said. She looked about to say more, but at that moment Maxie started crying.

"It's so horrible!" he said.

"You're safe now," said Harmony.

"You don't understand!" Maxie said. "There's someone else down there. Down in the darkness!"

"Who?"

"I couldn't see. But I could sense him. He just sat there across from me, not saying a word. I—I didn't even hear any breathing."

There was a silence, the kind that comes after a thunderclap.

"Time to get Mom," Bro said.

TWENTY-EIGHT

ARTHUR

I T'S NOT SO EASY TO SLEEP WITH LOTS
of commotion going on, but I'm pretty good at it.
Clinging to sleep is one of my best talents. Did that
mix with a career in law enforcement? Why wouldn't it? I
wriggled around a bit on the warm grass, closed my eyes a
little tighter, made my mind as fuzzy and foggy as I could.
Which is plenty fuzzy and foggy. I'm kind of brilliant when
it comes to mental fuzziness and fogginess.

"Lydia—you all right down there?"

Hmm. That sounded like Sheriff McKnight. He and I
were pals of course, so I was happy to welcome him into
my dreams. But then came a click and a pop and a bright
light flashed on, way too bright, turning the insides of my
eyelids red. It was too much even for a champion sleeper.
I opened my eyes.

Uh-oh. So much to take in all at once. I prefer to take
things in slowly, one every couple of days or so. How was
I supposed to handle this?

First, it was still night, except around the wishing well,

263

where it was as bright as day. Second, there were so many people: Mom, Harmony, Bro, Maxie Millipat, the sheriff and some of his other deputies, the hard-hatted crew headed by Lydia—the woman who'd been in charge of digging up the tomato patch—although there was no sign of Lydia herself right now. And let's not leave out Queenie, perched on Harmony's shoulders. She looked at me. I looked at her. I knew what I wanted: to be on Harmony's other shoulder. I'd never been on Harmony's shoulder, or anyone else's. Why was that? As for what Queenie wanted, I had no clue.

Third, there was so much activity. One of the crew stood in the back of a truck, aiming a big spotlight on the wishing well. Another truck, of the cherry-picker type, was parked right next to the well. The sheriff stood by the cherry-picker platform, over the well, and a cable dangled down from the platform and out of sight.

"Lydia?" the sheriff said. "Say something."

From down in the well came Lydia's commanding voice. "Haul away."

A crewman on the platform moved a lever. A sort of grinding machine noise started up and the cable began to rise. Up, up, and then another platform came into view, a small platform with Lydia crouched at one edge, the white ponytail dangling from under her hard hat. Taking up most of the space on this platform was a figure, motionless and muddy,

264

who . . . who seemed to have a big red nose. And . . . and seemed to wearing the clothes of a clown. I barked. I didn't know why. The bark, very high-pitched, nothing like my normal bark, just came out of me.

"Oh my god," Harmony said.

"Cuthbert?" said Bro.

"Has to be," said Harmony.

The sheriff glanced over at her and gave a quick, tiny nod. Mom stepped between the twins and put an arm over each of their shoulders. Everyone's eyes seemed huge and black in the bright white light, like . . . like bits of the night no light could get rid of. Except for the eyes of the figure lying beside Lydia, which were closed.

More machine grinding and the small platform was lowered to the ground. Lydia stepped off and the sheriff went over to her. She looked at him and shook her head. They gazed down at the figure in the clown suit.

I found myself wandering over there, too, for no particular reason, and joined the sheriff and Lydia in gazing at the clown. A man, for sure, which I knew from his smell, human males and females smelling very different. There's also a smell that comes when a creature stops being alive. I wasn't picking that up, not exactly. Were his eyes open? No. Was his chest going up and down? No. I was about to have a thought or two about all that, but before those thoughts got started, I picked up the aroma of a certain kind of biscuit I like, coming from Lydia's direction. Wow! My nose was on fire tonight! Not really on fire, of course, which would be terrible. I just meant my nose was stepping up big-time. Not really stepping, of course, since noses can't just up and . . . and I forgot where I was going with this.

Sheriff McKnight knelt and placed his finger on the inside of the clown's wrist, held it there for a bit, and sighed. Then, very gently, he removed the red ball from the clown's nose. "Anyone here ever seen Cuthbert out of costume?"

People shook their heads.

The sheriff and Lydia's crew got busy, making a sort of yellow tape fence around the small platform and the well. The bystanders backed away. And there I was, all by myself next to Cuthbert, if that was who he was. I sniffed at him, then again and again. I picked up all sorts of smells—watery smells, muddy smells, smeared makeup smells—but what I did not pick up was that one certain smell that means the end. That was confusing. Sometimes when I get confused, I bark an odd sort of squeaky bark that doesn't even sound like me.

"Arthur?" said Harmony from the other side of the yellow tape. "What's wrong?"

I didn't know, which was why I was confused. Harmony ducked under the yellow tape and came over to me.

"Arthur? What are you doing?"

I seemed to be very close to Cuthbert, sniffing and sniffing.

"Arthur?" Harmony crouched beside me. She gazed at Cuthbert, then at me, and back to Cuthbert. I could feel her thinking, like something powerful was cranking up. She leaned forward so that her face was almost touching the end of Cuthbert's nose. "No breath at all," she said quietly. "So what are you trying to tell me, Arthur?"

I barked my squeaky bark.

"I read somewhere about this drowning where the cold water kept . . . ," Harmony began, maybe finishing the thought inside her head. Then she reached out, placed a hand on Cuthbert's chest, and pushed. Nothing happened. She tried again, pushing harder this time. Still nothing. Harmony tried once more, on her knees and with both hands, real real hard, hard enough to make her grunt and to hurt whoever's chest was getting pushed like that.

Cuthbert groaned. A soft little groan, but no doubt about it.

"Sheriff!"

TWENTY-NINE

QUEENIE

T HE SMALL PARLOR IS ONE OF MY favorite rooms in the inn, especially in winter, when Elrod builds a roaring fire. From the top bookshelf where the old paperbacks are piled—and there's nothing more comfortable than a paperback pile—I often pass a whole day just gazing into the flames and thinking deep thoughts, mostly about me. No fire now, of course, it being summertime. The night—maybe the longest of my life—was finally ending. Through the windows overlooking the herb garden—old leaded windows, the most beautiful feature in the whole place, according to Mom—came the first light of day, that weak milky light that only lasts until the sun comes up.

There's a long table in this parlor, usually pushed against one wall, but now in the center of the room. Sheriff McKnight sat at one end. Maxie sat two chairs down from him on one side. No one else was in the room, just the three of us. Nothing was happening, except for some twitching of Maxie's legs, first one and then the other. The sheriff sat very still, gazing out the leaded windows.

"Um," said Maxie, not looking at the sheriff, "what are we doing?"

"Waiting for your mom," the sheriff said. "I like to have a parent in the room when I talk to a kid."

Maxie got upset. "But that means she's going to find out!"

"A dead man got pulled out of that well, Maxie. Well, almost dead. And dead for sure if it hadn't been for Harmony, plus there's no guarantee the docs can save him. The whole town's going to find out."

Maxie's mouth opened wide. "Oh, no! Do you think I had anything to do with . . . with whatever happened to him? He was already down there when I fell in."

"How did you fall in?" the sheriff said.

"I guess I misjudged the holding power of the ground."

"Not following you, Maxie," said the sheriff.

"It was too soft, probably from the rain last week," Maxie said. "I didn't factor that in."

"Maxie?" said the sheriff. "How about backing up a little?"

"You mean about the tent pegs? They're ten inches long, so I figured they'd hold."

"What were they holding?"

"The rope ladder, of course. But I was only down a few feet when they gave way."

"And you fell to the bottom of the well?"

Maxie nodded. Both his legs were twitching now. Maxie gazed down at the table. The sheriff gazed at him.

There was something in the sheriff's gaze that reminded me of Mom. Very strange. I was trying to sort that out when the door, which maybe hadn't been quite closed all the way, opened, and in came Arthur. That, too, was strange. He'd never figured out how to push open a door that wasn't fully closed. Unless it was already open wide enough for him to pass through, he never came in, just stood there waiting for . . . well, who knew? And now, out of the blue, he'd figured it out? This was a new development. In general, I'm against new developments. Arthur walked in and stood next to the sheriff, standing rather tall for Arthur, his gaze, just like the sheriff's, on Maxie. What had gotten into Arthur? I'd only been gone for . . . hmm. The truth was I didn't know how long I'd been gone. That realization reminded me of my enemy, out in the world somewhere. I rose and paced among the paperbacks. Silently, which is my way. No one looked up. They hardly ever do.

The sheriff stood and looked out the window. "How long should it take your mom to get here?"

"The distance is two point seven miles so assuming an average speed of twenty miles an hour it would be seven minutes nineteen seconds, give or take. But there are unknowns—did she have to get dressed? Was there a problem with Captain Eddie? What if she's low on gas? She never looks at the gauge and—"

"Who's Captain Eddie?" said the sheriff.

"Our pet bird," said Maxie.

Ah, yes. Captain Eddie, quite a large bird, mostly blue except for some yellow tufts spreading from its head—and most important living uncaged at the Millipats' house. I'd once been taken there on a visit, but hadn't had the pleasure of spending any private time with Captain Eddie, just the two of us.

"Getting back to knowables," the sheriff said, "how come you wanted to go in the well in the first place?"

"I just don't believe in Magical Miranda," Maxie said. "That's the basis of it."

"Who's Magical Miranda?"

"A fraud, but I can't prove it. Yet."

"Not quite keeping up with you, Maxie," the sheriff said.

"Don't feel bad," Maxie said. "It happens all the time."

"With other kids, too? Or just adults?"

"Both."

"There's not even one kid who can keep up with you?" said the sheriff.

"Nope. Well, maybe Harmony. And Bro, too, in a weird way. But that's it."

"And what about Magical Miranda? Is she a kid?"

"Kinda. She guesses your weight at the county fair, and she's always right—like to the pound. That's impossible without some kind of trick, and I'm going to prove it."

"Why is it impossible?" the sheriff said.

"Because of science!" Maxie said. "And if those tent pegs had held, I'd have the proof already."

"Why is that?"

"Because I saw her throw a device into the well. That means she knows I'm hot on the trail."

"What sort of device?" the sheriff said.

"I don't know, exactly," said Maxie. "A body mass scanner of some kind, very sophisticated."

"How deep is it down there?" the sheriff said.

"Two feet, ten and a half inches," said Maxie. "Give or take."

The sheriff got on his phone. "McKnight here," he said. "Have we got a trained diver on the team?" He listened, a tiny frown appearing on his face, but vanishing right away. "But what happens if we have to search a pond or—" He listened again. "Lydia handles it? Okay, here's what I want you to do."

Then came some instructions. I might have tuned them out in any case, but at that moment I spotted a mirror hanging on the wall across from me. That was new. Mom must have hung it there. A brilliant idea. I could see myself perfectly without having to change position in the slightest. How good I looked! Amazing, after all I'd been through. I blotted out everything happening in the room, all the comings and goings, and simply gazed at myself and thought nice thoughts about ME.

■ ■ ■

A trance, if you like. I fall into them from time to time, just another fascinating fact about me. When I came out of it, kind of like waking from a lovely dream, I felt refreshed. I was still up on my paperback shelf. Sheriff McKnight sat alone at the table, two red balls in front of him. Clown noses, perhaps? Whatever was going on, clown noses had to be a part of it. I'd already figured that out by myself, and I hadn't made the slightest attempt to even bother trying. The sheriff moved the balls around a bit, then shifted them back to the way they'd been. I left out Arthur, napping on the floor, his head resting on the sheriff's highly polished shoes. The door opened and Harmony and Bro came in.

"Hi, kids," the sheriff said. "Take a seat."

The kids sat down.

"No news on Cuthbert yet," the sheriff said. He pointed to the table. "Two clown noses. This is the one Cuthbert was wearing. This is the one found buried in the tomato patch, presumably by Arthur." Under the table, Arthur's tail rose and fell with a soft thump. Almost as though he was following the proceedings. What an amusing idea!

"Your mom," the sheriff went on, "is pretty sure she saw Arthur running around the house with the second one in his mouth. Did either of you?"

The kids shook their heads. "But if that clown nose was in the house, what does it mean?" Harmony said.

273

"Whoa!" said Bro. "A clown was in the house?"

"Not in costume, of course," Harmony said.

"You mean a guest?"

"Maybe."

They both turned to the sheriff. "I'll want to go over the guest list with your mom," he said. "But meanwhile, what can you tell me about the photo shoot? Did the clown say anything?"

"Nope," said Bro.

"The lady from the cat magazine, Ms. Vance, joked about it," Harmony said.

"Oh?" said the sheriff.

"She asked if the cat got his tongue," Bro said.

"Yeah," said Harmony. She gazed at the two red balls. "By the way, his nose was green."

"Cuthbert's?" said the sheriff.

"Shouldn't we be saying 'the clown who took the pictures' instead?" said Harmony.

"For sure," the sheriff said. "Thanks for coming in. You've been a big help."

The kids stood up. They turned to the door, then paused and exchanged a look. "Maybe it's a pattern," Harmony said. "The cats get switched."

"And so do the clowns?" said Bro.

"Yeah," Harmony said. "So who is the green-nosed clown?"

"Any ideas?" the sheriff said.

The kids shook their heads again.

"If one comes to you, let me in on it," said Sheriff McKnight.

The kids nodded. "Come on, Arthur," Bro said.

Arthur thumped his tail again and stayed where he was.

"What's with Arthur?" said Harmony.

The kids left without him.

Not long after that, Lydia came in. She wasn't wearing her white hair in a ponytail. Instead it hung straight down, limp and damp. She set a small shiny object in front of the sheriff.

"What's this?" he said.

"The only thing in the well that came anything close to your description."

The sheriff picked it up. "A locket?"

"Open it," said Lydia.

Sheriff McKnight opened the locket and gazed at the small, circular photo inside. "Is that Randa Bea Pruitt, the lady from the fair?"

Lydia nodded.

"Who are the others?"

Lydia pointed. "That's her ex, Marlon. He's fighting her for ownership rights."

The sheriff looked closer. "I've seen him."

"You have?" said Lydia. "Word is he's run off with some other woman." She pointed. "That's their daughter, Miranda."

"Magical Miranda?" said the sheriff.

"Correct," said Lydia. "And one more thing. I also found this, down on the bottom." From her back pocket she took out a big, heavy wrench and handed it to the sheriff.

A wrench? Interesting. From the way he was studying it, I could tell that the sheriff thought so, too.

"Doesn't look like it was in water very long," he said.

"Agreed," said Lydia.

The sheriff rose. "Many thanks, Lydia."

"Just doing my job."

Lydia left the room. The sheriff put the locket and the wrench in a plastic bag he took from his pocket and followed her out. Then, from under the table, Arthur— who I'd assumed had settled in for one of his very long naps—sprang up and ran, or at least waddled rapidly, after them. He seemed to be going through a strange phase. An improvement or not? I wasn't sure.

I spent a few more moments thinking about Arthur, then glided down off the bookshelf and curled up on the chair where Harmony had been sitting. She really does have the nicest smell, for a human. I closed my eyes and drifted away.

■ ■ ■

Oh, what a deep deep sleep! I knew I was sleeping and was in no hurry to stop. I needed it! Hadn't I been through a lot? Way too much. But sleep was making things right. I felt them getting righter and righter and was very close to being back to normal, when I heard someone coming. Human. Male. These are things you can tell just from the sound. A somewhat familiar sound that . . . that I associated with unpleasantness.

I opened my eyes, the lids so very heavy. And there before me stood Marlon, my enemy, in his Mr. Ware disguise. A drooping, empty duffel bag hung over one of his shoulders, and in his hands he held a thick towel. I started to raise a paw, but sleepily, not with my usual speed. He flung the towel over me, wrapped me up, and popped me in the duffel bag.

I tried to claw free, tried to cry out, but I couldn't move at all. And I could barely breathe.

Then came a voice, human, female, somewhat familiar.

"Excuse me. I'm looking for Maxie."

"Maxie?" said my enemy.

"My son. He must be around somewhere."

"Can't help you," my enemy said. "I'm just a guest."

Her footsteps faded away. The inn got very quiet. It was me and him.

THIRTY

ARTHUR

WE ROLLED AWAY IN OUR COP CAR, me and the sheriff. He spoke on the phone, possibly with Randa Bea, although I was too busy watching out for bad guys to pay much attention. What did bad guys look like, exactly? Like that old dude headed slowly out to his mailbox? I stuck my head out the window and gave him a bark he wouldn't soon forget. He jumped, almost right off the ground. A bad guy for sure.

The sheriff glanced at me. "Arthur? Some problem?"

Just bad guys roaming around our town willy-nilly, but other than that we were good.

We stopped at a red light and the sheriff gave me a longer look. "I wish I knew what you know about red nose number one," he said. "I get the feeling you've solved the case already."

How nice of him! Sheriff McKnight was my favorite sheriff by far. Were we going to pull a uey and cuff the old guy at the mailbox? That seemed like the next move but it didn't happen. No problem. It was still early in the day. We would probably fill the car up with cuffed bad guys by lunchtime.

The sheriff's phone buzzed. "Hi, Doc," he said. He listened, his hand tightening on the phone. "A blow to the head?" he said, and listened some more. "He didn't hit it at the bottom of the well?"

I heard "No" from the other end. My ears are good at picking up the other side of phone calls if they want to. "He went in feetfirst—both ankles are broken. He was already unconscious. A blow to the occipital lobe was what did it, guaranteed."

"Like a blow from a wrench?"

"A big one, possibly. Why?"

"What's it going to be, Arthur?" the sheriff said. "Back to that cabin in the woods?"

Sure! Why not?

But after a silence, the sheriff went on. "I have a feeling our bird will have flown that coop by now."

We had a bird? News to me, but I was still a newbie in the law enforcement game. I looked forward to meeting our bird sometime soon.

Not long after that, we turned into the fairground parking lot and went all the way through to the end. An attendant in a bright yellow vest swung the gate open and we drove on where no other cars were allowed, all the way to the ticket booth. This was the career for me.

Randa Bea and Magical Miranda were waiting for us. They both looked not too good, their faces pale and tear tracks on their cheeks.

Sheriff McKnight pointed to a picnic table. We went over and sat down, except for me. I stood right behind Randa Bea and Miranda, ready for . . . well, for anything. No flies on me, as Elrod often said about himself. At that very moment, I felt one land on my tail, but I flicked it right off.

"Thanks for meeting us," the sheriff said.

Randa Bea and Miranda glanced around, as though looking for someone else. I had no idea why. People get confused from time to time. You've got to cut them some slack.

"Cuthbert's still alive but unconscious and the docs don't know if he'll make it," the sheriff went on. He turned to Miranda. "Your mom must have told you what went on last night. We're now pretty sure that someone knocked Cuthbert out and threw him into the well."

Randa Bea put a hand over her mouth. Miranda did the same.

"We're going to find whoever did it," the sheriff told them. "But I need your help."

"Anything," said Randa Bea.

The sheriff laid the silver locket on the picnic table. "This was at the bottom of the well."

Randa Bea leaned forward and opened the locket. "Oh my god!" She turned to Miranda. "What . . . what's going on?"

Miranda's huge dark eyes filled up and overflowed, although she made no crying sound. "I'm sorry, Mom."

"But . . . for what?" her mom said.

"It was a lie."

"I don't understand."

Miranda jabbed her finger at the photo in the locket.

Randa Bea laid her hand on Miranda's. "It wasn't a lie when it was taken."

"But now it just teases me." She glanced at the sheriff. "That's why I threw it in the well." She reached into her pocket and took out a small silver coin. "I'm keeping this instead."

"A nickel?" said Randa Bea.

"Bro gave it to me—for making a wish." She put it back in her pocket.

"Bro was with you at the well?" the sheriff said.

Miranda nodded. "I'd gone to visit Harmony, but she wasn't there. Bro was picking tomatoes. He showed me the well."

"Did you see anything unusual?" the sheriff said. "Signs of a struggle?"

"No."

"Anything in the well?"

"It's so dark," Miranda said. "You really can't see anything."

The sheriff pointed to the man in the photo and turned to Randa Bea.

"Is it true he's fighting you for ownership of the company?"

"Did Yvette Reddy tell you that?"

"It was someone else," the sheriff said.

Randa Bea sighed. "Yes, it's true. There are no secrets in a place like this."

"Not sure about that," said the sheriff. "We're dealing with a big secret right now."

"The secret of who attacked Cuthbert?" Miranda said.

"Exactly," the sheriff said. "Whoever it was switched places with Cuthbert sometime before the beauty contest. Was the attack then or later? That's still a mystery. But I am pretty sure it was all about the cats."

"How do you know all this?" Miranda said.

"Harmony and Bro figured most of this out," the sheriff said. "I just listened." He stood up. "But Bro never said anything about you throwing the locket in the well, Miranda, so I'm going to run it by him."

Miranda teared up again. "I didn't let him see that."

"Fair enough," said Sheriff McKnight. "But I double-check

everything. In this business, you've got to put yourself in position to stumble into a good clue now and then. You're welcome to come along."

Stumbling was important in law enforcement? My career was going to be off the charts. I was so happy about that that I hardly minded when Randa Bea took the front seat. I sat in back with Miranda and did some first-class law enforcing, barking out the window at a bad guy carrying groceries and another one on a skateboard.

"You said it was all about the cats," said Randa Bea as we passed the village green, meaning we were close to home. "Can you explain that?"

"Well, specifically about Queenie," the sheriff said. "Someone wanted her very badly."

"Why?" said Randa Bea.

"Oh, Mom," Miranda said. "She's beautiful."

"So beautiful someone just had to have her?" Randa Bea said.

"There's a long history of people stealing beautiful things just to have them," the sheriff said. "Although in this case I think there's more to it than that."

"Like what?" said Miranda.

"That's a missing piece," the sheriff said. "But you don't need every piece to solve a crime. Sometimes even just one does the trick."

We all thought about that, me for hardly any time at all because I had no clue what he was talking about. I peered out the window, waiting for bad guys to appear. None did, but as we got close to the inn I did spot a red car parked off the side of the road under a big shady tree, a tree I knew well from having peed on it many, many times. A woman sat behind the wheel, gazing straight ahead. She had short, very light blond hair and wore deep red lipstick and cat's-eye glasses. Hey! Pamela Vance! Not a bad guy, so I didn't bark. The sheriff turned into our driveway and we parked in front of the inn.

As we got out of the car, the front door of the inn opened and out came old Mr. Ware. He had a suitcase in one hand and a white duffel bag over his shoulder. That was a lot for an old man to carry, and he was moving extra slow. Then I remembered how he wasn't actually that old and got a bit confused.

Bro and Harmony stepped out behind him, carrying a whole lot of what looked like bike parts. They saw us and moved our way. Mr. Ware shot us a quick glance and came to a sudden but very brief stop. Then he continued on, walking stiffly down the driveway.

"Who's that?" the sheriff said.

"A guest," said Harmony. "He just checked out." She turned to Miranda and said, "Hi. You all right?"

But Miranda didn't seem to hear her. She was watching

Mr. Ware make his way along the driveway, her face changing in a way that's hard to describe, maybe on account of so many feelings suddenly happening inside her.

"Dad?" she said, very quietly.

Everyone turned to her, worried looks on their faces. She didn't notice.

"Dad?" she said again, a little louder this time.

"Miranda?" said Randa Bea. "Oh, dear. Miranda?"

Miranda didn't hear that, either. She started moving down the driveway.

"Dad? Dad? DAD!"

Mr. Ware, now almost at the end of the driveway, looked back. A breeze ruffled his wild white hair. His face, too, went through some hard-to-describe changes, and ended up looking scared.

"Dad! Dad! What are you doing?" Miranda called.

"Oh my god," said Randa Bea.

Mr. Ware spun around and started running, not at all like an old man. His wild white hair flew off.

"Halt!" the sheriff shouted. "Police."

But Mr. Ware did not halt. He kept running to the end of the driveway and then darted down the road. We all started running after him. Mr. Ware turned out to be surprisingly fast. By the time I got to the end of the driveway—in the lead!—he was almost halfway to the big, shady tree. The red car pulled onto the road and sat there, the engine running. I started to huff and puff a bit, despite how speedy I'd turned out to be at this stage in life. First the sheriff passed me, then the twins, but I kept ahead of Miranda and Randa Bea.

"Halt! Police!"

"Dad! Dad!"

Sheriff McKnight was sprinting now. He reached down as though to draw his gun, but ended up leaving it in the holster. He began gaining ground, a real fast runner himself, which was what we expect in law enforcement. Mr. Ware glanced back and ran harder. The sheriff closed in, got within tackling distance. But just as he was about to launch himself, Mr. Ware pivoted and swung his suitcase with all his might. It hit the sheriff right in the head and he slumped down on the road.

Whoa! Mr. Ware had done that to my boss? I got so angry, angrier than I'd ever been, and in my anger forgot all about huffing and puffing. I ran my very fastest, even faster than I had at the Frisbee contest. Mr. Ware ran, too, closing in on the red car. I charged after him, catching up in great bounds. He reached the car, grabbed the handle of the passenger door, and flung it open.

"Go! Go! Go!" he shouted to Pamela Vance.

The car began to roll. Mr. Ware swung one leg inside, started to raise the other, and—

And nothing! Because with one last bound, I caught

him, sinking my teeth deep into his leg. Well, more like just his pants, but I had a really good grip on them.

"Go! Go! Go!"

The car sped up, with Mr. Ware half in and half out and me holding on to his leg and never letting go. He twisted around, tried to punch me in the face, missed, and tried again, launching a tremendous blow. At the same time the car started to spin out. Mr. Ware lost his balance and went flying out of the car, as though that punch was taking him with it. Since I still had him by his pant leg I went flying, too. We landed on the side of the road. Mr. Ware hit the ground hard and went right to sleep. I landed in soft grass and didn't feel a thing! The white duffel bag thumped down right beside me, the side splitting open.

The red car kept going, the passenger door hanging open wide. The sheriff came running up, blood all over his face.

"Halt!" he yelled at Pamela Vance. "Halt!"

She did not. The sheriff drew his gun and fired a single shot. There were two bangs, close together, the bang of the gun and the bang of one of Pamela's rear tires blowing out. The red car came to a stop.

Mr. Ware sat up, rubbing his head. The sheriff snapped cuffs on him in one smooth motion, click click. Harmony, Bro, Miranda, and Randa Bea came running. There was lots of crying and shouting and commotion and in the middle of all that something started moving in the white duffel bag.

Out from the hole in the bag stepped Queenie. Daintily? I think that's the word. She didn't really look at any of us, just yawned and then climbed up into Harmony's arms and gazed into the distance, those golden eyes glittering.

We law enforcement types don't expect a lot of thanks. Just doing our job is enough.

Although a treat would be nice.

THIRTY-ONE

QUEENIE

THERE'S SOMETHING ABOUT SUN-
sets that makes humans quiet down a little, a good
thing in my opinion. We have good sunset views
from the patio, which was where we all gathered at the end
of that busy day. By *we*, I mean me, Mom, Harmony, Bro,
Miranda, Randa Bea, and Sheriff McKnight, a bandage on
his forehead. And Arthur. There's no leaving out Arthur.
That was clear to me now.

The talk was all about the case, and the case was all
about me, specifically my beauty. I knew all there was to
know about my beauty, so only tuned in from time to time.

"Pamela made a full confession," the sheriff said. He
faced Randa Bea. "She claims that when she met your—
when she met Marlon, he told her you were already
divorced. By the time she learned the truth she was, quote,
too far gone."

"Uh-huh," said Randa Bea.

"It was Pamela who found out about this scientist
named Dr. Park," the sheriff continued. "He's overseas

somewhere, possibly in an uncooperative country. At this point it's not clear what we could even charge him with, supposing we could find him and bring him here. He's a biological researcher of some sort, supposedly brilliant, and he's developed some new techniques for cloning on a huge scale. Kind of like genetic mass production."

"He wanted to make millions of Queenies?" Harmony said.

"Maybe not millions, but many," the sheriff said. "But first he had to find the perfect candidate."

"Queenie," said Bro.

Millions of Queenies? What a terrible idea! There is only one.

"Apparently the initial animal doesn't survive the process," the sheriff went on. "Pamela heard about Queenie from someone at the magazine and Marlon came in the spring to check her out."

"May eighth—it's in the register," Mom said. "Is that the reason for the disguise?"

The sheriff nodded. "As for Cuthbert, Pamela says Marlon never intended to hurt him. He tried to give him some knockout drops—evidently the same kind he injected Queenie with—but they got into a struggle and . . . and Marlon picked up whatever was handy, which happened to be the wrench. I don't believe that part, since the attack took place in Cuthbert's trailer and we've got a scan of a receipt showing Marlon bought the wrench in Sarasota,

Florida, last March, meaning he had it on him when they met. Marlon assumed Cuthbert was dead and hit upon the idea of hiding the body in the old well. All this is from Pamela. Marlon's not talking."

Bertha came out with sandwiches and drinks plus yet another sausage for Arthur. He'd been snacking pretty much nonstop for hours.

"Miranda?" Harmony said. "Feel like a bike ride?"

Miranda, who'd been staring down at the patio floor, said, "That would be nice, but I don't have a bike."

"You can ride on my handlebars," Bro said.

"Yeah?"

"No problem," said Bro. "I rerigged them."

"Kinda," Harmony said.

They laughed, first just Bro and Harmony, and then Miranda joined in. They went off and not long after that I spotted them biking across the meadow, black silhouettes against the fiery sky, Miranda's silhouette perched up high on the handlebars.

Randa Bea went inside to make some calls. That left me, Mom, and the sheriff. Plus Arthur, lying on one of the padded chaises.

The sheriff looked at Mom. "Is there anywhere we could go to talk about Arthur out of his hearing?"

Mom laughed. "How about a little walk?"

They went for a little walk, side by side, in the direction

of the herb garden. Just before they rounded the corner of the house and vanished from view, their hands almost touched. Hand-holding is one of the very best things humans do. Were Mom and the sheriff about to hold hands? They rounded the corner, so I couldn't tell you.

Right after that, the phone rang inside the inn. No one picked up. Then came a voicemail-type voice.

"Mrs. Reddy? Is the sheriff there? This is Dr. Adomakoh down at the ICU. Please tell him the patient is awake and breathing on his own." Click.

I walked over to the padded chaise, glided up, and lay down between Arthur's paws. One of his eyes opened. Did he look alarmed? I had no problem with that.

ACKNOWLEDGMENTS

Many thanks to my very talented editor, Mallory Kass.

ABOUT THE AUTHOR

Spencer Quinn is the pen name of the Edgar Award–winning novelist Peter Abrahams. He has written many books for younger readers, including the *New York Times* bestselling Bowser and Birdie series, the Edgar-nominated Echo Falls series, and the Queenie and Arthur series. His novels for adults include *Oblivion*, *The Fan* (made into a movie starring Robert De Niro), *The Right Side*, and the *New York Times* bestselling Chet and Bernie mystery series. He lives with his wife, Diana, and dogs, Audrey and Pearl, on Cape Cod, Massachusetts.

READY FOR MORE ADVENTURE? GET YOUR PAWS ON THESE CAN'T-MISS MYSTERIES FROM SPENCER QUINN!